The Bee & the Fly

The Bee & the Fly

The Improbable Correspondence of

Louisa May Alcott
&
Emily Dickinson

Lorraine Tosiello & Jane Cavolina

Copyright © 2022 by Lorraine Tosiello & Jane Cavolina

ISBN: 978-1-955904-03 2

Published by CLASH Books in the United States of America.

www.clashbooks.com

Cover and interior design by Matthew Revert

www.matthewrevert.com

To my husband and family, who tolerate it all—Lorry

To my friend Lorry, who asked me who my favorite poet was—Jane

Bee! I'm expecting you!
Was saying Yesterday
To Somebody you know
That you were due —

The Frogs got Home last Week —
Are settled, and at work —
Birds, mostly back —
The Clover warm and thick —

You'll get my Letter by
The seventeenth; Reply
Or better, be with me —
Yours, Fly.

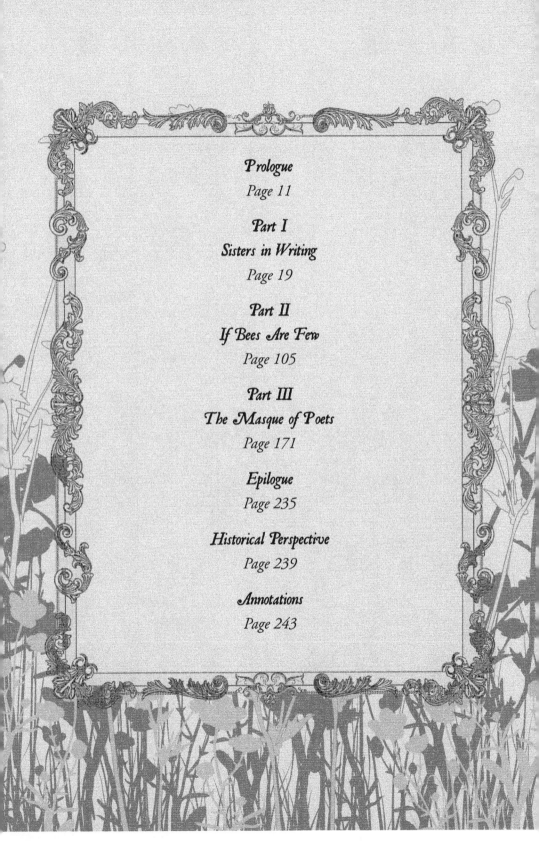

PROLOGUE

I am at the desk again today, because there is nowhere else to feel at peace. Outside the window, the snow-drifted street should be silent, but there are two trucks parked in front of the house. One seems to be a local news van. A young woman in a beanie and parka is braving the weather, filming in front of the house. I recognize her as the correspondent of all things cultural on our town cable station. She must be talking about the conference that will start tomorrow in Amherst. The letters are being showcased to American-literature scholars for the first time. After six months of vacillating, tomorrow I will know what the experts think.

The other van has its motor running. I recognize George in his red puffy jacket. George comes every few days and waits for me to leave the house. Then he accosts me with a friendly grin and asks if I have changed my mind. He wants to come in and scan the attic for ghosts. He has a video camera and a bright flashbulb and says he can get his hands on an electromagnetic field detector, if things show promise.

I slide open the creaky door to the concealed compartment of the desk. It's empty now, but I have to convince myself that it still exists. Six months ago, it yielded up its treasure. I will never forget the faint, old-fashioned scent that wafted from the hidden recess: apples, blancmange, and plummy buns, the tumbled aromas of a warm and boisterous home, the output of a greathearted spinster. It was followed by the fragile bouquet of roses, sweet peas, nasturtium, and lemon verbena, pressed flowers from a sweet garden, the legacy of a reclusive and passionate gardener.

My hands swipe the empty cabinet and I feel bereft. A lingering doubt, as if I have betrayed my sisters, haunts me every day.

The packets of letters—one tied with a sturdy brown cord and the other with a satin ribbon of the palest lavender color—charmed me. Then I opened them. One set was written mainly on blue lined paper in a hurried scrawl, efficient words and little attention to punctuation; the second, scribbled in petite letters on scraps of paper, often in pencil. The penmanship had a decided rightward slant, large spaces between the words, and dashes the predominant punctuation mark.

I was in my father's attic in Lexington, Massachusetts. I work in a bookstore in Concord.

I know this handwriting. I know these women.

I moved to my father's house when he started to fail. As the oldest daughter, with no spouse or children to relocate, I was the natural choice. We spent the time perusing old scrapbooks and photo albums and recollecting family traditions. Once Dad accepted that he would never regain his stamina, we were able to close down his workshop and distribute his last pieces as he directed. A meticulous restorer of antique furniture, Dad had loved his connection to the history of Lexington and Concord. He regretted the pieces he would never rejuvenate.

I had never lived in this house before coming to nurse Dad several months ago. I entered into the daily trial of responsibility and worry, duty and heartache in an unfamiliar spot, but that suited me. I had been a wanderer, a nomad, ever since I left my family home to go to college. Three years would pass and I'd begin to chafe, eager to live in a new city or just to have a different view out my window. Now, with every day, the pull of home and the bonds of family tightened. I thought of the cozy creation of my childhood favorite, Louisa May Alcott, who nearly invented the picturesque lure of home life right in neighboring Concord. Family compounds abounded there, the Emersons, the Hawthornes, the Thoreaus ensconced in the familiar.

Dad's care was not difficult, nor particularly sad. I took him to his radiation treatments. Afterward, we would stock up on groceries. Bread, bananas, milk.

It was essential to him that these were in the house at all times and in ample supply. On good days, we walked a few paces outside, his walker a better support than I could be. On bad days, he slept on the couch, and I read, did laundry, read, made unending pots of stew and rearranged the freezer to fit it all, and read.

My brothers were either impossibly hopeful or seriously oblivious to the needs and urgency of Dad's situation. I longed for a friend to turn to, not so much for help, but for sympathy and comfort and womanly understanding. I started an unanswered correspondence in my head with wise women I found in books, from Queen Isabella to Isabel Archer, and accepted imagined advice.

But it is hard to get your head past the mid-nineteenth century when you are surrounded by the ghosts of revolution, literature, and philosophy. I had spent my long visits at Dad's appointments trying to appreciate the moldy essays of Emerson and imagining Thoreau as a rock star. There are worse ways to keep a vigil.

After a month or so, I began working at the bookshop in Concord. I have always been a reader. My first book was, of course, the Fun with Dick and Jane Reader. I would stand at my father's knee and practice my homework: "Bow wow! Bow wow! said Spot," I would proclaim. My father would shake his head and say, "It's Bow *wow*! Bow *wow*!" I guess that's when I learned that there is more than one way to read a story. The first novel I read was *Little Women*. I like to think that its heroine, who kept her dearest treasures in a tin kitchen in the attic, prepared me for a most amazing discovery.

The old wooden-framed windows were wedged shut, swollen in the heat of an August afternoon. The slant of light that poured through the narrow dormer opening only highlighted the dust I had just churned up. No wonder I was coughing and sneezing. It was my own fault that I was alone in this sweltering attic on a sunny summer day.

When Dad died, my brothers were helpful with the details of the funeral arrangements, the financial issues, and the real estate negotiations. But sorting through the relics of Dad's life, that fell to me. "That's so depressing," they'd say, or "Just fling it, it's worthless," or "Dad didn't want us to be going through his stuff."

"Fine! I'd rather do it alone," I said and tramped up to the attic to do my work in solitude. It wasn't that I expected to find any heirlooms, or that I needed closure, I just wanted to reminisce about family ties, to sort through the things that he had accumulated—the odds and ends that, in the end, represent a life.

I had already shuffled through the generic stash of paperback novels, coins (carefully sorted in plastic pill bottles, by year and denomination), the Hess truck collection, and the meticulously ordered boxes of baseball cards, arranged by team and date. I had stopped to pore over Dad's famous baseball newspaper clippings, all carefully entered into a scrapbook, everything in it about the New York Yankees, from Mickey Mantle Day to Derek Jeter Day, the secret of his obsession with the rival team sequestered away. The stamp collection was kept in equally precise order. Books were another passion that Dad and I both shared. He had a veritable library of poetry anthologies, complete works (tending heavily toward Walt Whitman, surprisingly), and even clippings from literary magazines. When I was in college, I shared some poems of Emily Dickinson and we both struggled with their otherworldliness. He used to irritate us as children when he would recite poetry to illustrate a family moment. Invariably it would run toward "The Charge of the Light Brigade" or Joyce Kilmer's "Trees." We would respond ungraciously with, "I do not like green eggs and ham, I do not like them Sam I am." Though books are among the hardest items for me to part with, they would have to go to the library's fundraiser.

All the neglected tools of his furniture restoration trade came next: scrapers, spatulas, saws, chisels, planes, hammers, rulers, calipers, tape measures, clamps, paintbrushes, sanding blocks, screwdrivers, wrenches, and files. Though Dad had relinquished his business, he had not been able to part with the gadgets that helped him turn industry into art.

All this I sorted and assigned to family, auction, dumpster, or Goodwill.

I straightened my glasses and wiped the sweat off my brow. I squinted past the small pool of light to the far end of the gable. This attic had nooks and crannies extending in rays from the center of its big old eighteenth-century core. It didn't look like Dad had ever been to that musty end of the attic. Varied chairs and headboards, of eclectic styles from colonial to midcentury, were waiting to be refinished, nearly obscuring the way to the edge, of what? I shifted a few empty frames, mismatched chairs, and some old tennis racquets. A larger piece of furniture was behind all this rubble, partially blocking the only window toward that end, casting an ambiguous shadow. It was covered with a densely begrimed swatch of sturdy fabric and seemed isolated from the rest, as if it had been in place long before the ruckus of my father's enthusiasm overtook the attic.

Now, this is getting interesting, I thought, as I lifted the worn, ancient linen cover. The sheet itself had a notable weight. It was cream colored, closely woven, with hand-stitched hems. The stitches were tiny and precise, as if made by a young girl determined to tame her own spirit, or a small woman intent on savoring the details of daily existence in her pristine work. In one corner, there was a hand-embroidered spray of flowers, and a monogram, an elaborate N. We had heard that the old house had been owned by a family named Norcross, and I wondered if this was a relic of their posterity, not mine.

I was expecting to find a spare Colonial chest, or a practical Transcendental bookcase, the legacy of our locale. Instead, I stared at an elegant Victorian lady's desk. It had spindle legs of deep walnut and a delicate frieze of lotus leaves across the top, ornamentation that reflected femininity. Within its yard width, it was part bureau, part rolltop desk, part vanity table, and it was topped by two small, accessible shelves. There was a petite but usable mirror, brass knobs, and inside, a green leather desktop. I had never seen such an exquisite and personal piece of furniture, designed to lighten a woman's chores, provide beauty as well as function, and serve as a store for her dearest belongings. I caressed the range of cubbies and pigeonholes inside, feeling the timbre of its quality and history in the very grain of the wood. I felt like Thoreau about to release his desk to the sunshine and free wind, to remove it from the dust and care of its many years. I remembered one of Dad's happy moments, when he found a series of secret compartments and drawers in a historic desk he was restoring for a client. There were no gold doubloons or unsettled wills found there, but the surprise and satisfaction of solving an ancient puzzle was a reward in itself. I am sure it was he who guided my fingers to the back wall of the cubbyholes and simultaneously to the sturdy wood of the back of the desk. My two hands were three inches apart. There was a secret space in this desk. Could Dad have missed this?

The tambour of the desk had rolled open with a gentler motion than I expected, given its age and years of abandonment. A soft layer of dust covered the magnificent green leather desk surface, which slid out from under the tiny drawers and niches that covered the back wall of the desk. One corner of the leather seemed to have been pried open sometime in the past, and then shabbily replaced. Someone had either been hiding or looking for something in this desk. Perhaps they had missed what I had discovered, that the back of the desk held a false chamber. Or perhaps they knew. Even assuming its existence now, it would be difficult to enter that chamber without damaging the cabinet, the wood dry and fragile, brittle from decades of garret heat. There might be a latch or a spring in one of the drawers, or somewhere under the leather surface. I wondered whether such a mechanism, if it existed, would still work. I was thirsty and my water bottle was empty, the heat made me slightly dizzy, and I couldn't stay in that stifling place much longer. I lowered my head, closed my eyes, and leaned heavily on the front of the extended desktop, thinking. I sucked in my breath as the wood creaked beneath my weight. With that sudden downward force, I heard a click. The surface held my weight, but I felt a gentle pliancy that I didn't expect. Holding on tight to the leather desktop, I was able to glide the writing surface of the desk forward over a catch. I supported the wood and leather surface as I pulled it forward, removing it completely. Once it was dislodged, the cubbyhole portion was free to slide forward. It was heavy and it groaned but it came out in one piece. Behind was a simple wooden partition, which shifted open with a woeful screech.

I sequestered the letters, devouring them again and again, and withheld judgment. I studied the paper, the ink, the expressions, and the content. From what I had read (over and over as a girl, as a student, and now as a sleuth), they seemed authentic to the authors in every way. I heard the moralistic yet boisterous voice of one woman and the visionary song of the second. The two voices comforted me in the long nights after my father's death. I started to believe.

I looked at documents in the famous libraries—Houghton, Fales, Concord, and the universities. I compared handwriting. I searched bibliographies and indexes. Nowhere in any of this scholarship did the paths of these two women cross.

I accosted a famous Dickinson scholar after a lecture in Amherst and peppered him with questions. How was Emily Dickinson, the recluse, connected to Thomas Wentworth Higginson, Helen Hunt Jackson, and Thomas Niles? The prevailing theories were less satisfactory to me then the simple connector of Louisa Alcott, who seemed the hub of this literary set. He pointed out that he knew of no material evidence to connect Emily and Louisa. Nothing concrete existed in the comprehensive collections he had examined.

I continued to vacillate. Discovery and revelation seemed to be exactly what these women renounced. They had taken care to keep their friendship clandestine. It started off tentatively. It was clear that they had every intention of having the letters destroyed. Yet their loved ones hesitated on that point, just as I did. The people they sought to protect were long gone and these letters could only illuminate, not dim, their story. With each reading I sensed a broadening of their achievements as well as a realization of the depth of their struggles.

Ultimately, a pilgrimage helped resolve my doubt. I visited one woman's home as the morning sun drenched through the high windows and revealed the brilliance of its inhabitant; I entered the second home to a warm afternoon glow resembling the embrace of a beloved family. Two literary reputations confronted me, two discrete Victorian ladies made me hesitate, but it was the voices of two true little women who told me that words of friendship, encouragement, and personal integrity should always be revealed. It was finally clear to me that Emily and Louisa were releasing their correspondence.

I make no claims.

In the end, the letters must stand for themselves.

Part I

Sisters in Writing

Lu's letters are so splendid we'll almost regret when she comes
home.
—May Alcott, 1862 letter to Alf Whitman

The Way I read a Letter's — this —
'Tis first—I lock the Door—
And push it with my fingers — next —
For transport it be sure —

And then I go the furthest off
To counteract a knock —
Then draw my little Letter forth
And slowly pick the lock —
—Emily Dickinson

A lifelong correspondence were a biography of the correspondents.
Preserve your letters till time define their nature. Some secret
charm forbids committing them to the flame.
—Bronson Alcott, Concord Days

Amherst

May, 1861

Dear Miss Alcott,

I fear that you will think me vain to write you and seek counsel without introduction. And vain perhaps in another way—to think you might assist me. I have but a poor few poems and wish to make them known. Two were lately printed here in Springfield, one just this May. I have read your story in the august magazine, and think perchance another lady would be so kind as to offer suggestions to "this little Rose — nobody knows."

E. Dickinson

The May-Wine
I taste a liquor never brewed —
From Tankards scooped in Pearl —
Not all the Frankfort Berries
Yield such an Alcohol!

Inebriate of air — am I
And Debauchee of Dew —
Reeling — thro' endless summer days —
From inns of molten Blue —

When "Landlords" turn the drunken Bee
Out of the Foxglove's door —
When Butterflies — renounce their "drams" —
I shall but drink the more!

Till Seraphs swing their snowy Hats —
And Saints — to windows run —
To see the little Tippler
Leaning against the — Sun!

Concord
May, 1861

Dear Miss Dickinson,

As I have only just begun to sip the wine of fame, after ten long years of fermenting the grapes, I fear I may be the wrong person to be of assistance to you. I suppose the "august magazine" you mention is The Atlantic Monthly, and having placed two stories there in the last year, I *do* have some satisfaction that I have finally reached a pinnacle.

Having deliberated on your questions, I realize that I may have a bit of advice for a sister writer, if I can know your desires. I suppose you know already that poetry, such as yours, is generally printed anonymously. Does this suit your purpose for "making them known"? I ask this because I have often written anonymously myself as I have had to alter my stories to suit my purchasers. I can write a sentimental tale, a moral story for children, a patriotic poem or a serial where the heroine goes mad and the villain gets entombed alive. I won't say I'm not proud of my work, but some has been hastily written to suit the market. The stories are lively and tell of conflicts and misunderstandings between real people, not just pirate battles or adventure plots that fill the gazettes lately. I'm practicing my writing for the real work that lies ahead. Though I alter my style, I never lower my principles and my villains will always be deceived, dishonored, ruined or poisoned in the end.

I'll write anything that sells, but my greatest fun was when the first story was printed and I read it aloud to my favorite audience, my dear family. How they hollered and cried when they found that their little Lu was a published authoress! Does your family rejoice in your talent too? Now I keep it up to pay the bills. How I love to have my scribbling turn into boots, bonnets and briskets and help to keep my family afloat.

Can I ask if you require ready payment, or can go without your just wages? As the money is important to me, I have learned that if the publisher thinks I am a man, I can get more for my stories, so I send them anonymously or with only my initials. I started out years ago getting $5 per story, but get a neat $25 for four pages now. The Atlantic takes a poor fellow's tales and keeps 'em years without paying, and as my principal aim is to pay the coal bill and keep my family shod, I often have to forego the honor and send my stories elsewhere.

Poetry is not my line, but I admire Emerson's most, though the public has crowned Longfellow. Your poem seems sprinkled with fairy dust and reminds me of my first book, "Flower Fables," which had a very small success. Your feminine style would not move Clapp at the Saturday Evening Gazette, as he seems not to understand a woman's sentiment, having rejected two of my honest stories with a woman's view. Leslie and his Illustrated Newspaper wants only the most lurid tales, and Elliot at the Flag of Our Union is going in for the military and patriotic, as seems necessary right now.

If you have a book of poetry, perhaps Mr. Briggs who published my "Flower Fables" would be interested. For getting printed in a periodical, the Atlantic is the best and as Mr. Lowell is the editor, your poetry will have an honest critic. If you like, I can send your poem on to him with a recommendation, should he remember my two little offerings which he accepted.

Though I cannot give you more practical help than the offer above, I feel that you and I can provide ballast to each other's ship as we "sail across the Atlantic." Forgive me for this long scribble, half advice and half raving. I am mad to know how other women manage their work — how do you write, as I imagine you have the same drudge of housekeeping as the rest of the gentler half of America. I long to know what inspires you, what books do you read & etc.

Write again so I know how you get on.

Very truly yours,
L. M. Alcott

Amherst
July, 1861

My dear Miss Alcott,

I'm afraid my long silence may have offended you — though it was not so still in my heart and mind. I have considered again and again how to answer you, the words just out of reach, then formulated responses rejected on the morrow. So though I have not written to you in these two months, a lively correspondence was held in my room. I can hear already your words to me: Say yes. And so I shall, with my most sincere and kindly thanks. I am moved by your generosity in my behalf.

I do not mind if my name were not to appear with my work. I would like the poems to be known, but care little if I am. It would mean to me that they are worthy and may perhaps be enjoyed by readers. Nay, I think I would like it better to remain unknown, so much I fain to lose the life I have, confined as I am now, only by the bounds of my imagination. The more known, the less free.

You asked about my family. My sister, Vinnie, is helpful to me. She takes on many of the domestic duties rightfully mine so that I may have the time and peace to write my little songs. She is my dearest companion, though I do not read to her, nor my family, as you do. Our family is different than yours.

I would have a quarter of your ebullience, though what I would do with it I cannot say.

Your devoted ED

To see her is a Picture —
To hear her is a Tune —

To know her an Intemperance
As innocent as June —
To know her not — Affliction —
To own her for a Friend
A warmth as near as if the Sun
Were shining in your Hand.

Concord
August, 1861

Dear Miss Dickinson,

I have received your little note with the understanding that you would like me to forward your poetry to The Atlantic Monthly, with an introduction.

It seems that since I last wrote, the champion of literature at the firm, Mr. Lowell, has decided to leave the position. As you may know, he has been instrumental in making this publication the leading beacon of new and important literature. His position has been taken over by Mr. James T. Fields. Mr. Fields is a worthy successor and I have had some encouragement from him. In fact, my second cousin Annie Adams is his young wife, and I happen to know that she gives her nod to some of the editorial decisions, so she may put in a good word for each of us. Why is it that fifty years after Miss Austen has flayed the conventions of society, it is still necessary for American women to have a male patron in order to be recognized and published? <u>Must</u> we pretend that only the men know what is for our own good?

It may happen that I will have to return to teaching this winter, as my governess position has fallen through and my writing does not pay enough to keep my family clothed and fed. To make matters even odder, I will be boarding with Annie and Mr. Fields while I work at the kindergarten. It all seems rather queer as the city is filled with rich relations, yet I drudge about looking for both shelter and work. I won't outright shake my manuscripts under Mr. Fields' eminent nose, but I can leave them in a conspicuous position. What I wouldn't do to finally become a famous author! I have changed, shortened, and inverted my stories to fit the whims of the publishers. Some day, I may write straight from the heart, a true and real story and see if that doesn't make me a fortune of my own!

I suppose we Alcotts are already famous for building castles in the
air. You say that your family is not like mine, but to describe the joy and
pitifulness that really defines our Pathetic Family could well take a whole
volume. I will give you a glimpse of the characters that I alternately want to
smother in kisses and strangle in exasperation.

Imagine a father as serene as an infant, as impractical as a philosopher
and as wise as a sage; optimistic to a fault and as useful as an umbrella
in a tornado. Beside him, sheltering him in her broad embrace, my dear
Marmee, who grinds and works so that he will be free to think and
converse. I do believe every great thinker needs a help-mate just like her.
It seems that you may have one in your sister, Vinnie. Is it your pet name
for Lavinia or is her name something more exotic, like Vincenza? Does she
really give you the time to think and write and protect you from daily cares?
I wonder who will ever give me the quiet I need to think?

It seems that Marmee's second greatest wish is to keep us girls together,
and her final purpose is to cheerfully share whatever little we have got with
beggars, downtrodden women and runaway slaves.

We used to be four sisters, and what a lively time we had with plays
and tramping and huckleberrying. Now, Nan has chosen to marry a poor
man (and shirked her responsibility to the family, some would say), Lizzie
has transmuted into the angel she always was (a more content creature you
never saw), and "little May," who towers over us all like a golden goddess,
gets her way in all things, studies art, and keeps above the daily grind.
Meanwhile, "wild Louisa" (ready to go off like a torpedo at a touch) bears
the burden of scrubbing along for the needs of the old folks. How I wish I
had a brother to help carry this worldly worry about warmth and woolens.
Do you have a brother? I imagine that must be the jolliest and most
comforting thing of all for a young lady. Not having one, I wear the boots
in the family and march forward to make my fortune.

You mention that your family does not read together. Let me tell you
how curious my family has always been on that point. When we were

young, our parents conceived that by putting our feelings and thoughts into words, we might perfect our characters as if writing alone could save our souls. They pored over the phrases in our journals and made helpful suggestions. Can you imagine having your own thoughts exposed, every evening 'round the fireside? If my journals ever outlast me, be assured that there will not be a true thought there. Do you think I would have let my own disappointments and worries add to the burden my mother already carried?

I feel that I can reveal more to you, a sister in scribbling, than I could to my own anxious, hopeful parents. As I have lost my sister Lizzie (my conscience) to scarlet fever and my sister Anna (my confessor) to the holy malady of matrimony, I would like very much for we two to keep up a correspondence.

Yours, truthfully
Louisa M. Alcott

P.S. Please do not let my bluntness alarm you. Though your words are gentle and precise, I suppose that would be more from prudence than prissiness. You will respond, won't you, Miss Dickinson?

Amherst
September, 1861

Dear Miss Alcott,

What an odd duck I must seem to you, we differ so in our ways! I could not write such a long and affecting letter yet what joy to receive such a one. Let me whisper that when I am the most loquacious I use the fewest words.

I thank you for your news of The Atlantic and for offering my poems to them. How you navigate those waters I cannot say — another thing I could not do. But I am grateful that you are able and willing to speak in my favor. (Miss Austen to the side, even in our day "Mr. George Eliot" must assume more than a masculine champion, but a masculine posture to be seen truly.) When you speak of the changes you have made to be acceptable to your publishers, I cringe for you and rethink my own meager efforts to be known. But I suspect no matter your concessions, your true heart lies within your work — and begin to think that you delight in impugning your stories. True or no, it is cheering.

Your family is a tempest! And how well you fit with them, full of thundering energy! You do not wish to have a brother. It is neither jolly nor comforting. But a brother's wife, that is a fine thing. And a sister, who indeed sacrifices much to protect my material and spiritual comfort. I hope that you will not miss yours overmuch while you are teaching, but am pleased that our fine friendship — may I say that? — will be unaffected.

I have no poem for you today. These last thoughts unrest me.

Your devoted
Emily Dickinson

Concord
September, 1861

My Dear Girl,

I realize that I have no idea if you are a young lady or an elderly spinster, but having read your last thoughts, I place you among the quiet, dutiful ones, who regardless of age, are relegated to keep their peace in the shadow of their august, all-knowing male protectors. Excuse me if I am wrong, but I sense that your brother (you did not tell me his name) has been neglectful of your genius.

Can I paint a picture of him? Let me see … he is quite educated and therefore <u>knows</u> much more than you, he is about in the world and therefore <u>understands</u> its motives more than you can ever fathom, he <u>rules</u> his family as is his right as a full-blooded lord of creation. From you he expects fidelity & compliance — he demands cheerfulness & adoration — he is surprised at your boldness & tramples your independence. Do I know him, Emily? Do not be surprised. I am an author. I have studied human nature and the society that rules it all my life. Excuse my punctuation, you can see that the subjugation of women gets my blood up. Rejoice that this brother is not your husband for then your legal right to your own voice, your own <u>being</u>, would ever be in doubt.

I look to my own practical and burdened mother and then at my mystical, unencumbered father. She whispers to me, "Why are men such icebergs when beloved by ardent natures and surrounded by love-giving and life-devoted beings? Why does he so much take, take and so little Give! Give!" At a young age, I had as an example a father who placed all his hopes in "The Family of Man" while his full-blooded family of women seemed less to him than the pure ideals he was seeking to realize. While we wanted for firewood, he built a picket fence to beautify our property; though he would not labor for pay, he built Mr. Emerson a whimsical summer house for their evening musings.

When I was a child, there were times when our family seemed near extinction with cold, worry and want, and then, how I hated him! Making Marmee and me, with our dark hair, our impatience and our hot tempers, the devils of the family, always wanting us to change our natures and bend our will to his resigned, hopeful, ridiculous philosophy. While improving my soul, he neglected my poor, shivering, hungry body and squashed my high spirits. "Be more like Anna, she does her lessons and obeys her parents." "Be more like Lizzie, she accepts her trials and never complains that she needs new shoes." (Nor would she, she didn't run in the woods every day to escape the lunatic and get some peace!) "Oh, and by the way, Louisa, if you exercised your mind the way you do your limbs, you would make far better progress."

We followed him and his ideals to a new way of life and nearly perished. Oh, those dark days at Fruitlands, when he took to his bed! When he languished in his room, defeated, diminished, how I wished he would die! I was a child, angry and hungry and tired, and he was the cause of all our family's misery. But as each day passed and I saw the crazed, hopeless look on my Mother's face, I realized that if we lost the philosopher, I would never have my Marmee back sane and serene.

That's when I saw the worth of my Father, through my Mother's eyes.

When he accepted that he did not have Utopia on this earth, he only had Marmee and me and the others, a poor substitution, then, like so many other quiet, dutiful men, he shouldered his responsibilities, all that was left him when the dreams fled. Some thought him mad, some unprincipled. Even the most kindly thought him a visionary whom it was useless to help till he took a more practical view of life. Even we, his family, often misjudge and reprove him, for he seems to live by a higher law. In many people's eyes he may seem improvident, selfish and indolent. Still so, he seems in my own at times — I wish he were more like other men.

I cannot tell you even now whether he is a sage or a fool, saintly or just stubborn. He has begun to achieve his little bit of recognition. We do not understand his metaphysics but set him gently on his path as he attends his "Conversations." I perform the coronation-ceremony with his best hat, May reties his old-fashioned neck cloth, and Anna runs to slip the beautifully written notes into his pocket, which he never needs to discourse in the very highest realms. Marmee smiles and encourages us to be all in all to each other, and everything to him.

You can see that discussion of my father riles me, as I assume your brother does you. I am glad that you have a dear sister and a sister-in-law with the sense to overcome her husband's shackles. You will rely on those womanly supports all your life.

Your sister,
Louisa

P.S. I trust you will destroy this letter. I would not want my father's detractors, nor his friends ever to read these confessions.

Amherst
October, 1861

Dear Louisa,

I laughed at your portrait of Austin Dickinson, it is so complete. You have said everything he would say if asked, but alas no one does, so we are spared hearing aloud the atmosphere that shapes his relations with all but Father. It is rather like not being here, and Vinnie, bless her, aids me in truly not being here, but spending much time in my room with my paper and pencils, or in the garden, observing life and all its passion and beauty and despair.

I will be ashamed later to have written this, but I feel I can unburden my heart to you in this. He is rather like a train, moving forward, full of noise, belching smoke, unconcerned — nay, unaware — of his effect on anything to the right or left of his track. Of his sisters and mother, he takes little notice. His wife, a measure more. That in itself is not what wounds me, but more the disregard of the poet at his feet, as he criss-crosses Massachusetts to be in the company of what he might find next door to his.

Would that we could sit and chat. I should like to console you in your hardships with your father.

I have put your letter where no one will ever find it, but cannot put it to the fire. Alas, someday they all shall be, together.

Your devoted friend,
Emily

Boston

November, 1861

Dear Emily,

Rather like not being here" — you have hit the nail on the head. Our fathers, brothers, even lovers look through us, don't they? As if we do not have the same thoughts and yearnings, as if we are a different beast. It seems that they are confusing what we <u>do</u> with what we are <u>capable of</u>. On any morning, we set the bread to rise, the beans to soak, grind the coffee and sweep the hearth — all before they are called from their paper. While our heads have been in the pantry theirs have been to the stock exchange and the Halls of Congress.

And yet, even though he thoughtlessly looks for us to mend his jacket and dust his top hat, my father never tired of educating us girls — not a traditional education, but one that emphasized morals and good habits and the love of learning. How I wish I could have attended college! My sister Nan and I were teaching school before we ever finished our own education. I do think that college men think they know everything, can do everything, have everything. <u>Life is my college</u>, my writing, my thinking, my observing — getting all I can from lectures, books, and the good people around me. Mr. Emerson had helped me ever so much through his careful recommendation of books, and generous reading of some of my early manuscripts. I am so anxious about showing him my "treasure," a novel I have been reworking for several years. Not only Mr. Emerson, and Mr. Thoreau, but my dear Mother has been an example to us by striving to learn and be all she can be, with her whole mind and heart. Clearly, all the philosophy in our house is not in the study; a good deal is in the kitchen, for high thoughts and kind deeds go well with the cooking and scrubbing.

So it is that Austin disregards your mind. I can see him at his society soirees, settling with the gentlemen in a den at the bottom of the house

— the densest particles always sink to the bottom, you know — and politics, cigars and brandy are generally nonconductors of lightning. I don't imagine your brilliance has struck him from that vantage point.

Does your sister-in-law take her husband's part or yours? I am glad that Vinnie is all to you that a sister should be. I hope that you share your work and books and sweet talks and that they are equal parts table linen and theology, prosaic duties and good poetry.

One can discuss Greek poetry and chop meat, and the one ennobles the other. Let me go now, my father requires his tea.

Yrs truly,
Louisa

Amherst

December, 1861

Dear Louisa,

I fear I may have been unjust to my brother.

How I admire the ease with which you state so boldly things which I turn around in my mind, and turn again, and so until I name its — essence. When I try to do otherwise, I err. There is much — all — truth in what you write. Yet it is wide of the mark, which is my father.

He is as full of fault as your dear father, though of a different kind, and unabsolved by better qualities. He does not comprehend us. And so cannot sustain us in our endeavors. He finds my "reveries" — his word — ridiculous. Austin told me that Father put on his spectacles to read them, but they were of no help, and that he didn't think "a telescope would have assisted him." It is not that I seek his approval, only that it shows discordance where one would hope for concord.

You see that Austin is more sympathetic, even though it goes no further. All I said of him was true, yet that too missed what lies beneath. He is perhaps more a victim of the Master's tyrannies. It sets him outward to seek a life more harmonious to his inner longings — whilst I go deeper inward. I can be myself entire only in a few places out of Father's circle, in my room, in the garden. So my brother and I miss one other as we pass in different directions in the same pursuit — me hither and he yon.

Tell me what you think, my friend.

Yours,

Emily

Boston

January, 1862

Dear Emily,

You speak so quietly but truth thunders from your words.
Already, you have named my biggest flaws — my impetuous
spirit and oh! my abominable tongue! Forgive me for
misunderstanding and writing thoughtlessly of your brother when I knew
so little. It is just that it never — never — would have occurred to me that
your own dear father would stifle you, and worse, criticize your desire to
write. We are a houseful of women and my father has never yet trodden
on our independence. More than that, when I am in my vortex, the family
gives me a wide berth and tiptoes about offering comforts of tea and apples
and cider until I emerge with my manuscript. Then there is a general whoop
of joy, everyone congratulates me, tells me it is the jolliest story they have
ever read, and looks forward to the necessities it will provide.

But your family don't seem to want to encourage each other. Not
that that is so very odd — I have noticed that half the human race seems
to make a mess of their domestic relations. In our family, most of the
disrespect and misunderstanding comes from without, for we Alcotts cling
together, labor for each other, and never utter a harsh word in public. I
believe we would actually have perished if we had not all pulled in the same
direction. As Marmee says, we each do our part alone in many things, but at
home we work together, always. And though we have little, we were always
rich in home-love.

And so you say that you withdraw, quietly, and refrain from argument,
and get peace in your own way. Some girls are taught to control themselves,
an early lesson and often learned too well. But I imagine you as a fluttering
moth, circling ever inward toward the brilliant flame you create in the

center of your own home. I won't say that it doesn't baffle me when a young woman finds all she needs in one particular home. Our Lizzie was a content soul, who saw her whole world in our family circle, and was so gratified by an evening with us by the hearth that I wonder that she is not homesick for us even in heaven. Perhaps you are a creature such as she.

I feel restless and anxious to be always seeing, doing and learning more than I am. I need the world, the creatures in it, every bloom, every odor, every sly glance, every rumbling carriage to fill my stories. I am wild about new adventures, and some day I will travel to Europe, see Goethe's house and the Globe Theatre and snow on Alpine peaks. Aren't you keen to get away? When I am home more than a few months, I chafe to leave. I need my independence and I <u>will not</u> be confined. How can you find your comfort and all that you desire in one place? Is home really that warm and safe?

Yrs,
Louisa

Amherst
February, 1862

My dear friend,

Your picture of your family is such a lovely scene, it cannot be real! Yet I know it is. How different our lives are! And not. I touch such a life with Vinnie, though in hushed tones, and sometimes with Austin, when he is not afield on his own quest.

I fear I could not thrive in such a way. I would not know how to live with it. That life, I think, is over there. I can see it through the door that opens on your world.

It is in the quiet where my thoughts bloom — in the dark where my candle shines, and by whose light I make my little songs. To answer your question, it is not all warm and safe, but it is home to me — the place where that flame lives whose light I am by nature drawn, like your moth, tho' it burns at times. When my august father stands at the gate, I wonder whether walking out is necessary, and decide not. This sends me deeper into myself, my room, the garden, and closer to that candle.

I am so grateful that you let my thoughts spill.

I have written a little poem for you.

With affection,
Emily

A Moth the hue of this
Haunts Candles in Brazil.

Nature's Experience would make
Our Reddest Second pale.

Nature is fond, I sometimes think,
Of Trinkets, as a Girl.

Boston

February, 1862

My dear Emily,

Wartheye are turning out to be much the same, it seems, the more I know of you. So you, too, are mystified by the thoughts and actions of your father. I am sorry that he is something of an ogre (can I say that?). You must keep any letters about him well hidden. You seem to have a lot of confidence in your hiding spot. I like to destroy my evidence. When I was fourteen, in my Romantic Stage, I wrote some love letters to Mr. Emerson. Thank goodness I had the good sense to destroy them!

I have learned that I have to bottle up my anger and my stormy thoughts, or I would be spouting all over, all the time. There was more yeast put into my composition, I guess, and after standing quiet in a warm corner so long, I begin to ferment. My mother has helped me with my volatility and wretchedness all my life and encouraged my writing as a safety valve for the steam that I work up. I can't stop myself from writing. Well, we must each be what God and nature makes us. We can't change it much—only help to develop the good and control the bad elements.

People say I have a forceful, fiery kind of exterior, too, and that I have rather a masculine air. Folks think I am blunt and abrupt, but I only mean to be honest and sincere. I cannot tolerate shams and mindless courtesies. People are put off by my tall, gangly body, my mass of chestnut hair, my cold, steel gray eyes. If I look rough it's only to hide my tender heart which wants to explode at all injustices in my path. Tell me how you look, Emily, or send me a photograph, if you have one.

It seems that I was born with a boy's nature, fight my fights with a boy's spirit and rail at life with a boy's wrath. I am wild to go South and do something. They may be getting up a school for the Negroes in Washington, and I hope that I will be asked to go. I want to get as near as I can to the action. How is it that your brother is still at home, when the Massachusetts 27th has set off for the front?

Ever,
Lou

Amherst

February, 1862

My dear Lu,

Horrible, horrible events. Two editors came today. Mr. Fields must have sent them. I did not know, I was not ready, but nothing could have made me so. They cared not about what I'd put to paper, the observances I knit so carefully to convey — even tho' so few see them — my letters to the world. They bartered as if for flour or tea. How can you fare well in this world?

Publication — is the Auction
Of the Mind of Man —
Poverty — be justifying
For so foul a thing
Possibly — but We — would rather
From Our Garret go
White — Unto the White Creator —
Than invest — Our Snow —
Thought belong to Him who gave it —
Then — to Him Who bear
Its Corporeal illustration — Sell
The Royal Air —
In the Parcel — Be the Merchant
Of the Heavenly Grace —

But reduce no Human Spirit
To Disgrace of Price —

    I will remain unknown and happier be — committing to paper what Nature tells me, and to hands I cannot see.

Em.

Boston
March, 1862

Dear Emily,

Forgive me if this paper is spotted with salt water, but your poem has moved me deeply and I hardly know how to reply. With a few stabbing words you have revealed not only your terror, but my compromises — and with a sigh and a dash have exonerated me due to my poverty. Thank you for understanding my — <u>our</u> — struggles as no one else possibly can. My family revels in my success and the comfort it brings them, the editors care for nothing but their circulation, paying more for lurid stories than anything with a moral. Preserve your dignity, Emily. I, more than others, understand the impossible position in which the world places an absolute idealist. (As I have told you, it is my duty in life to support one.) If you have both the integrity and the <u>means</u> to protect your thoughts, your work, your very self, I congratulate you. We are not so very different, for I, too, will remain anonymous as long as my work makes me less than proud. If posterity remembers me only for these rubbishy tales, I will be mortified.

Now, as I am fierce and practical Lu, I will give you a suggestion. First, I regret being the medium that brought Boston's literary monthly men down on your head in such an insolent fashion. I am used to their brash confidence and bow down to their suggestions, but you, dear, are ready to try to your hand at greatness and that cannot be sold. I understand your indignance, for I, too, have been humiliated by Mr. Fields.

As you know, I had nowhere to turn for employment this winter, but to my friend Mrs. Peabody who encouraged me to open a kindergarten using her educational methods. Mrs. P. and my father have been associates since they worked in the Temple School together. Mr. Fields gave me $40 to furnish the school and offered his patronage. As if it is ever necessary for a woman to have the protection and approval of a lord of creation! Having no brother, nor husband and a father who needs we four women to give <u>him</u> protection from reality, I have been forced to tolerate being a beggar at the home of Mr. Fields and his wife. It is remarkable what false positions poor women can be forced into.

The school has been dismal. Though the children get on, I have no patience, and I have not been able to percolate my stories as I wished, a wasted winter. My dear sister May has offered to complete the term at the school and I have already returned to Concord and written a story which made me more than all my months of teaching. When Mr. Fields heard I was leaving, he said, "Stick to teaching Miss Alcott, you can't write." I need nothing more than that charge to set me grinding even more, to prove that I <u>can</u> and <u>will</u> write, see if I don't!

Since he has taken over The Atlantic, the mighty magazine has become dreadfully afraid of certain words and ideas. They rejected one of my stories for fear it would inflame the feelings of the Southerners! Were they disturbed by your punctuation, Emily? They are so very proper, it's a wonder they don't remove themselves to Concord, home of the staid.

If you still desire to have your poetry read by a literary critic, I implore you to let me contact our friend Mr. Higginson. I assure you he is a man of utmost integrity. He is a sympathizer of women's causes and a great mentor to young writers. I have known him since I was a child, as he has been a great supporter of the anti-slavery movement. He is kind and honest and learned. I suppose that he will treat you carefully.

If you only knew how many times I was rejected and scorned by publishers, you would understand why I feel that every trial and criticism teaches us something. We can only keep scribbling, keep up our long & patient labor, through uncertainties and disappointments, that is the only drill needed.

Your companion in scribbling,
Louisa Alcott

Amherst
April, 1862

   Have written and pray he
tosses it in the fire, but dream
he answers me.

Concord
April, 1862

Bravo Miss Emily!

You have written to Mister Higginson! You are a saucier
spinster than I imagined — and I like that! Now we await his
benediction — or ban — or befuddlement. Let's not let the
good editor know that we are in on this together. I shouldn't like to impede
his astonishment at your lovely verses, nor diminish his gallant patronage.

I chuckled at your mode of announcement — scribbled on that little
scrap of paper as if _you_ half considered committing it to the fire instead
of sending it off to me. Is that how you compose your lines? Jotting bits
onto nearby scraps, before the inspiration passes, or words fail? It reminds
me of something my father noticed at Mr. Thoreau's. (He no longer roams
the wild woods, being confined to his mother's home, and accepts our
visits willingly.) Henry used the very invitation which my mother sent
requesting him to attend the wedding of our dear Anna and John — as
a convenience to note down some musings on fruits. This way of writing
fits Henry's style. His life is so simple, paper so dear, and his mind so
overflowing with wise thoughts.

As rough and ready suits Henry's style, you can imagine that the
erudition and eloquence of Mr. Emerson's writing comes from a truly
serene and elegant chamber. His shelves are lined with superb editions of
Shakespeare, Dante, Goethe and the great philosophers. In fact, he owns a
heavy crystal drinking bowl with Gothic letters, given to him by Carlyle,
which is said to have belonged to Goethe. From that magnificent possession
to a poignant one, for on the wall hangs an Italian picture once belonging
to Margaret Fuller. How I cringed before it when I was a child, for it was
salvaged from the fateful wreck that caused the death of her entire family,

still showing the marks of water stains. So inspired by his heroes, he reposes in a fine, grand room that suits his thoughts.

As for myself, you will find me at Apple Slump, enrobed in my glory cloak, scribbling mightily with a jug of my father's hard cider nearby (it makes the lurid stories flow that much truer). I think out sketches of stories and put them away in little pigeonholes in my brain for future use. I spend the entire week, whether in front of those tiresome kindergarteners, or sewing blue shirts for the boys, spinning tales in my head, 'til they need to get a vent somehow and then I scratch them out in one huge vortex and be done with it. I've taken Mr. Emerson's lesson to heart, "The way to speak and write what will not go out of fashion is to speak and write sincerely." I try to have my people speak exactly the way we really do talk. Why search for the perfect word when the simplest, truest, most natural are the best? This is my method and it works for right now, I have two books half done, nine stories simmering, and stacks of fairy stories mouldering on the shelf.

In the end, I think it is not so important where and when we write but how and why we do. A manuscript locked in a mahogany desk is not worth more than one locked in my rusty tin kitchen in the attic or in the secret place where you stash your poems. The goal is to unlock them, somehow. I'd like to lay off exotic maidens, delirious villains, leprosy and intrigue, but these tales are easy to write, folks like 'em and they pay into the Alcott Sinking Fund. But some day, I promise you, I will write what I have truly seen and keenly felt. I will write something that I can put my name to. Maybe Mr. Higginson can help you unlock your secrets, too. He's an advocate for all beings downtrodden and I think you is downtrodden, too. If you won't enter the limelight, you are bound to be illustrious some other way.

Yours in ink,
L. M. Alcott

Concord
May, 1862

Dear Emily,

I suspect you have heard the news already about Henry Thoreau's death.

It is hard to bear the thought that Mr. Thoreau has left us just when the ideals he strove for, even risked his life for, are about to be tested and vindicated.

The hero of my youth is gone. Let me tell you a little of what he was to me. A teacher, of course, for whom the wide fields, the deep forests and the flowing river were his classroom. A man of total integrity and strength of intelligence, and such local color and candor, that my father calls him "our ruddiest and noblest genius." He was a stalwart friend of our family — he stood among the few at our Nan's cozy wedding, carried Lizzie's coffin to her shady rest, and stood by my father when others doubted his worth.

He was the first man who ever saw me as more than a "female child," but as an individual intellect, equal to any man in feeling and knowing. I learned to love him dearly — his passion, his sensitivity, his unyielding righteousness. He never was what ladies call handsome, but for me, his serious eyes, with his pure, true heart shining through them so clearly, that was beautiful to me.

Though the townsmen wondered why he absented himself from our proceedings, it was Henry who was one of the first responders the night that Sanborn was to be hauled away by the Federal Marshals. It was he who knocked down the driver of the coach and rolled in the dirt with him struggling to get away a loaded whip. How heroic he was that night! How much his ideals were expressed, as always, in his actions!

He had spent the most part of this year perfecting his death, in the same way that he sought to purify, simplify, and improve his life. The whole town, it seems, has brought him flowers, fruits, fish and their farewells. Mr. Shepard, the town jailer, who had become a great friend since the night Henry spent in jail, said he never saw a man dying with so much pleasure and peace. His savage stare has long since stopped disconcerting our townsfolk, they no longer thought him peculiar for examining a trout or a wren for hours, and though he wore the worst boots in town, all agreed his soul was of the highest order.

Mr. Emerson likely overstepped his authority by having Henry's services in the church, but his eulogy was true to my hero's worth and when my father read some of Henry's own words, I think he convinced many of our dear teacher's essential faith.

I think of you in your little kingdom, asking for nothing outside your own sphere, your absolute devotion to your own individualism, and I see that you could be Henry's equal in living a pure life. It seemed never his point to achieve fame, he was aiming higher at truth and wholeness.

And then, what of myself? I am always plunging forward in my topsy turvy way, to make a mark, or prove a point, or make a great gesture. Still, perhaps, my time is now. I've always wanted to live in stirring times, to have a part in great deeds, to earn some of the glory or the martyrdom.

I <u>must</u> do something other than sit at home sewing shirts for our boys. I'd do anything to be close to where the action is. I am a "fighting May" and my blood is up. I'm casting around for a way to go the front, as a nurse, a cook, a scribe or whatever slot I can fill. There's nothing I wouldn't try to help to put right this great wrong.

It seems a fitting way to honor my mentor whose legacy calls to me, "Action from principle, the perception and the performance of right, changes things." I'm ready for change.

Yours,

Louisa

P.S. I will be the one to send a little bit of poesy this time. It's still "fermenting" and not complete, but I am sketching out a tribute to Henry.

Haunting the hills, the stream, the wild,
Swallow and aster, lake and pine,
To him grew human or divine —
Fit mates for this large-hearted child.

P.P.S. You have not told me if you heard from Higginson yet? He is getting up an infantry regiment and is sure to move out to action sometime soon.

Concord
May, 1862

Dear Emily,

Have you read Harriet Prescott's "The South Breakers" in The Atlantic this month and last? It's better than Prescott's usually are, being more natural and simple. Still, there is something in it that seems too flawed for my taste. Her indirect, swarmy style and her women who seem to act only on intuition, unexplained religion, or blind devotion to love seems dangerous to women's integrity. I'd rather have them act because they <u>understand</u> the danger, not have a <u>hunch</u>, and they <u>know</u> the consequence of their actions, not <u>hope</u> things will work out.

Her feminine style makes me wonder if there <u>is</u> a difference between the writing of a man or woman. In the same issue of The Atlantic, Miss Dodge comes out from her façade as Gail Hamilton and announces, "I am a woman!" and then, "Men will neither credit my success nor lament my failure, because they will consider me poaching on their manor." Is there a place we can call our own instead? I am always aspiring to be Shakespeare, Dickens, or Emerson ... while maybe Brontë should be my guidepost.

They say that "your" Mr. Higginson has become a great patron of Miss Prescott ... what say you about her writing?

Louie

Concord
July, 1862

Dear Emily,

I have sent letters with no response from you that I wonder if I have offended you with some offhand remark, if you are troubled with our communication or if you have so many other witty, sage and interesting correspondents that simple Lou's letters are the last to get answered.

Then, I worry that you have some trouble, and how would I know, dear? Perhaps it is time that you told Vinnie about our friendship, just so she would let me know if you needed me. I have no comparable being to confide in on my end. May is much too self-absorbed and would only notice if I, myself, stopped writing to fill the coffers.

So write please and tell me if you are in your volcano spewing poetry, or if the lava is smoldering about something I said or if ash is belching and cooling down our once fiery communication.

Write soon to your loving friend,
Louisa

Amherst

August, 1862

My dear friend,

Nothing has occurred amiss, Lou, only the agitation of the mind that comes of thoughts of my father, who would be my master, and those men, and my poor brother, all of which oppress me so I cannot think or dwell in mine own habitat of the bees. It is not safe there in the world beyond my room. I find it — what they call life — a distraction, an interrupter that keeps me from God's purpose — to find some little way to make my true Master glad — not these earthly wretches. When I am a daisy — I bend my smaller life to his — and without this, I am lost, banished, guilty. Would they but leave me to my own.

Nothing indeed amiss, only a smoldering cauldron of lava!

I seek to go back inside, where I am happiest.

Thank you for your steadfast friendship.

Yours, Em

Concord
September, 1862

Dear Emily,

I shudder at your oppression and wonder if your father questions your mental faculties, and that you are thrown by his careless criticisms and worthless conventions into an "agitation of the mind." In this age, it only takes the insinuation of mental instability for a woman to lose her liberty, her place in society, her very self.

Still, your queer withdrawal from the outside world must come from a pitiful struggle within. Emily, I know something of the feeling that one's mind can be slipping away. I myself struggle at times with the blue devils. Once when I was young and alone and tired, I almost thought that it would be a relief to end my life. This terrified me, as my uncle Junius ended his life in a very deliberate and horrific way, and they say insanity does run in families. At other times I am in a vortex of activity that keeps me from sleeping, eating or stopping for days on end. Those days of activity are exhilarating and dangerous and full of power. It seems that the thoughts and voices of my characters are more real than the world I live in. My family accepts my moods and supports me through the times of intensity. Between those dizzy days of energy and those dreary days of despair, I am just Louisa, the drudger, the worker bee, perhaps, in your world of bees.

I have spoken to you before about the odd behavior from my Father. His philosophy renders him a quack to some, to others a fool, but some even say he is insane. And yet, Mr. Thoreau called him the sanest man and Mr. Emerson extols his conversation as sublime, so I can no longer care about the snickering from those who cannot soar with him. The high flights of his mind are essentially who he is and we can only honor and respect him. He remains the sweet and imperturbable man he has always and ever been, and that is the proof of his sanity: he is fearlessly and consistently true to his ideals. I know that you are not cracked, Emily. You are too straight and true to your own notions for that. It is sad that you are made to feel less than your brother, your father, or those men of business because of your purity of vision.

I cannot agree that withdrawing from the world is the correct path to take. It is ever true that the Lord our Master provides for the wild daisies, but the choicest blooms always seem to break through the clouds of mist and stretch their faces toward the sun.

Faithfully,
Louisa

Amherst
September, 1862

Dear Lu,

You are politic, my dear friend, acknowledging that I am not a broken jug — yet wondering whether 'tis wise to pour the milk in it.

I take no offense — there are many who think different, my own brother among them. Else why should he hesitate to make me known to his literary friends and associates. No, I am not a chipped vessel. I take my days as I do for there is the keenest possession of what has most meaning to me. I love this world, and it moves me to say things that are in my heart, and that makes me glad. I stay there because it is where I am most as I am, apart from, as Mr. Whitman wrote, the pulling and hauling (tho his poems are things I am meant not to have seen). If that is cracked, then I am cracked, like an old Sèvres cup. But I think not. My blooms grow well in this clime, though my garden is small.

I believe you understand because you have woven another kind of cocoon around your true heart, and I fear it never has a turn to speak.

Yours, Em

P.S. It is not that God provides — for — the wild daisies, it is that he — provides — them.

To make a prairie it takes a clover and one bee,
One clover, and a bee.
And revery.
The revery alone will do,
If bees are few.

Concord
October, 1862

Dear Miss Emily,

Y ou have gotten ahold of Whitman's opus and have it to heart I
see! Does your father know that you read the bawdy bard?
I remember the first time the book entered my home. Whitman
had sent the first little edition to Mr. Emerson, who found it extraordinary. He
brought it one evening to read aloud to my father, Henry and Ellery were there
as well, and Llewellyn. I have not told you of Llewellyn, but as he is the gnat
that irritates me the most in this story, I must paint him for you.

When we were young, and poor, and with only we four girls to entertain
each other, Llewellyn became a great favorite of my parents. He was an
orphan boy who was visiting relatives in Still River, where we hied after the
failure of Fruitlands, with our wounded pride, our lost fortunes and our
family badly bruised. My mother took an especial liking to him and he
boarded with us as a brother for many summers after that, in Concord, and
school times when we were in Boston. Though I had known and tussled with
many boys during my romping girlhood, Llewellyn was a more passive, girlish
boy. He played fairyland with us and took the parts in our plays that no one
else cared to do, and most especially, he sat by my father at night when the
Old Philosopher wanted most to weave his dreams and discuss his theories,
just when we girls were at a bursting point to have a good laugh or a quiet
read or a fiery argument, anything but listen to that tired philosophy.

So, because he listened, but most particularly because he was a boy,
Llewellyn would sit at the right hand of my father when Emerson and
Hawthorne and Sanborn and Mr. Thoreau would gather in the library at night.
"You remember Llewellyn, sirs?" my father would say and they would clap his
shoulder or shake his hand and immediately he was part of the venerable men's

club. It did not matter that he was an impostor, an ignoble initiate, an imitation, but he was present that night when they stealthily read the verses of "Leaves of Grass," leaving the four daughters off in the corner, sewing silently around the hearth, wondering about the whispers and the sighs.

Not much later, my father met Mr. Whitman on a trip to New York and wrote, nearly raving to my mother, "Walt, the Satyr, the Bacchus, the very God Pan … bodily, boldly, standing before us." That was all I needed to secret the little volume out of Mr. Emerson's library between two larger volumes one day. I thought I would find more of the "venerable men's club" but instead I found an intellect teeming with oneness of all of God's creation, more in the style of my beloved wild Henry than of staid Mr. Emerson.

Shall I repeat for you the lines that endeared me to him the most?

"I am the poet of the woman the same as the man
And I say it is as great to be a woman as to be a man."

Ever and ever, this is my motto. I swear I will do all that a man can do, but do it as only a woman can. I will control my destiny, I will earn my own way, I will not be judged by the shape of my bodice and some day I will vote, like a freeman in this country.

There is a cocoon that binds me, the one that all women are wrapped in, which forces us to appear only as a beautiful, delicate and ultimately doomed creature. I will not be that butterfly. I will be your bee, Miss Emily. I will traverse the whole prairie and sample everything that it offers, I will buzz and irritate the complacent and I will spin honey that pleases the masses and if I must sting to save myself I will do that, too.

And that gnat Llewellyn, the impostor, became a spiritualist, and was expelled from Harvard Divinity School for deception at a séance.

I never trusted him, from the first.

Your Bee,
Louisa

Amherst
November, 1862

Dear Louisa,

Your swirling gusts of steam and turbulence shake me. I see you thrusting headlong into the world, and bid you safe passage.

Here, my cocoon wraps me snugly and securely. I have my quiet place — or more, a quiet time — if not a space outside my little corner, where I write at night. Father agreed to it so long as it would not upset the household or my chores.

I sit quiet as a mouse at night and all the world breathes life to me. There is no sun to blind or wilt or expose me. There is no Time for I put the clock under a pillow and hear not its interruption, every minute. There is no daytime prattle — no excess of language filling the air.

When the night is darkest I see the most. How funny it must seem to you. Am I from the dark side? You must think me wicked!

But then the morning comes and I am the first to heed the clock. I set the bread to rise for mine is Father's favorite — and I breathe the fires to life — and I rattle the tea kettle so that all know the morn has come.

It is in the daytime that I am daughter and sister, baker and darner. And at night — what am I?

Good-night,
Emilie

Concord
December, 1862

Dear Em,

I've had enough of pricking my fingers on blue flannel jackets with the venerable ladies in Concord Town Hall, playing Dickens in the parlors of like-minded people, and selling pies to earn money for the cause — I've finally found a way to get into the midst of the action.

Mrs. Dix has changed the "age of consent" for going off to the front as a nurse. It's a comfort to know that at the ripe old age of thirty (which I passed last week, thank you) I am no longer considered either too innocent nor comely to go off to the bedside of our precious boys without being the cause of their fever or heartache. Emily, I am going to the front to nurse our wounded soldiers!

In our family, people have always seemed to like having me attend them, I've nursed plenty of friends and relations. The sorriest case of all was the uselessness I felt when our Elizabeth slipped away. I hope to be more helpful in this assignment.

Marmee is holding up so far. Mrs. Hawthorne has come over to mark my dreariest clothing with indelible ink. I've packed books and games, for I am determined to keep the dear boys jolly if not completely healthy. So, soon I plan to be watching the bright instruments without shivering, running for warm water, spreading salves on bandages, holding the smelling bottles, laying soft lint squares on wounds, and trying to look motherly and comforting while I quake inside.

It's a solemn cause, I'm glad to do what I can, and I'm sure the experience will do me good, whether I come out victorious or half dead with the effort.

I wait any day for my orders and you may not hear from me for some time.

In haste,
Louisa

Washington, D.C.

January, 1863

Emily,

I write to say that I am alive, despite the worried looks from doctors which give a body little encouragement. Every day, I spend more time delirious and I hardly know if it is the typhoid or the treatment.

Still, it is true (not just a figment of my fever) that I have won the $100 prize from Frank Leslie's Illustrated. My story was chosen from 200 submissions and will be printed later this year. Look for my "Pauline's Passion and Punishment" and don't cringe. Pauline is a worthy heroine filled with power over men, and after she demolishes several, accepts her punishment like a woman.

It seems too cruel that I should die now when I'm closer than ever to fame!

Yrs,

Lu

Concord
End March, 1863

Dear Emily,

The doctor said that I am able to sit near the window and write for a half hour today. I will rush this off to you, so that you know I am recovering.

Here's the line I send others, "Got typhoid fever and came bundling home to rave, & ramp, & get my head shaved." But Em, it was so much more than that. I was near death for weeks and rambling in and out of my wits. The wonderful visions were equal parts brain fever and laudanum. I went to heaven once, and saw such eternal do-gooders as Miss Dix and Dr. Channing, so I knew it was not the place for the likes of me. I even had a dream about you, locked in your room, and your Mother in the room above, whispering run, run, run! It's all fodder for the imagination and might do to churn into sensation stories.

It's rather solemn when you lie expecting to die, and your sins come before you, even though they are small ones. I felt such a sorrowful failure, for I had hardly done my duty before I was stricken, and carted away from the boys who needed me. I may have to pay dearly for the brief exposure, though, since I am still as thin as a rail and all my beautiful hair gone. My hope is that my mind isn't as far gone as my body. Tell me wits remain.

If I spend the rest of my life suffering from this illness, I will carry my burden proudly, for the bravery and humility I saw among the wounded made my sacrifice seem very small indeed. It will always be my proud badge of honor to have given a little bit of myself to the cause that I and my family have espoused and supported for decades. As my father says, he sent his only son to war. Would that I could have done more to bring slavery to an end.

My sister Abba May will be sniffing around to see who I write to with my precious little strength. She is convinced that I must have a lover from my experiences in Washington. Perhaps she will think that E. Dickinson in Amherst is one of the fellows I nursed, who would be indebted to me for saving his life, and of course, fall in love with me. Let's use that ruse for a while and keep her nose out of our letters.

Ever your admiring rack a bones,

Lu

Amherst

April, 1863

My dear friend,

No one could tell me of your health — and I could ask no advice — I worried you would succumb to a Minié ball as do our young men.

It is better to have you away from the pestilence — and eternity.

Ever,

E. Dickinson

Concord

May, 1863

Dear Emily,

Some of my letters from Washington have been printed in the papers as "Hospital Sketches," and the people are buying them up faster than they can be supplied. They find them witty and sad, real and sentimental all in one. I am not sure they are a very good thing, but I needed the money. Now, a publisher is asking for more and will print them into a book!

I am glad they find them heartwarming and gentle for I have left out the nauseating stench of foul wounds — the pitiful cries of the men gasping, retching and convulsing at the end of their lives — the horrifying sight of piles of limbs flung out the back door of the hospital — no one would surely care to read about that. I fear that I have glorified the men and the institution, because I so glorify the cause for which we fight. Nothing putrid should come from our noble aims.

Everyone seems to understand that Nurse Periwinkle, the slightly bumbling, energetic, naïve, but earnest young nurse is myself. I am writing another story with a different kind of nurse. Nurse Dane will be strong and courageous and righteous. That is the kind of story I wish to write and the kind of woman I wish to be. I want so much to write a grand and great, deep story, one that will be considered real literature.

I am having a bit of satisfaction and fun that the crowd likes my stories, finally. I'm not sure my "Sketches" are worth all the public believes them to be, but popularity is not a bad thing and will only help me when I finally finish my great novel.

Write soon,

Louisa

Amherst
June, 1863

Dear Louisa,

I stand numb by your sketches, should I speak, my breath would be all frost — I have no way to see what you have seen — my eyes are blind, my voice still, my hand stays listless, I lift no pen nor sword to meet your enemies.

My brother's friend was struck and left us — a bolt, from the wrong direction, for alas it brings no wisdom. Austin remains at home, my father paid for his safety and we are obliged.

You are brave, my friend, to bundle your anger and worry in a book.

I am not so, Bee,
Emily

Fame is a bee.
It has a song —
It has a sting —
Ah, too, it has a wing

Concord
November, 1863

Dear Emily,

I have got a letter from Higginson in South Carolina. He is now the Colonel of the First South Carolina Volunteers, an all Negro regiment. Oh, can you imagine the courage and commitment to the cause of righteousness? He is a man of thought & passion & action! Amidst all that danger, he read my story "My Contraband" and wrote to compliment me. He approves of both the realism <u>and</u> the ideals. With encouragement like this, I feel that if I stick to what I know and to my principles, I will get somewhere with my writing.

Has our conquering hero written to you lately? You are always so silent on that point. Does he give you good advice and have you taken it to heart?

Affectionately,
Lou over the Moon

Amherst

December, 1863

Dear Louisa,

You ask if Mr. Higginson is my new master. He has been as helpful as he knows how to be. He gauges if anyone would enjoy or even understand my songs. He advises that my style is unpolished, rough and unready for display.

This is useful, for I see him straining, stretching, and trying to approximate my view. He attempts to climb to reach my altitude but being mostly made of iron he cannot escape the pull of the Earth and tumbles back to terra firma.

While I — have learned to fill my lungs with pure air and my pupils dilate to let in all the light and so I soar a bit higher. I look back to Earth and see his disappointed face upturned and watching me fearfully — but he waves and I am encouraged and then he gets the bellows and keeps me afloat. This helps me, as you do with your wild energy and scattered, madcap adventures.

I need you both, even if Mr. Higginson only blows enough hot air that he nearly pushes me back, while you try to pull me forward with you — and each cancels the other — and so I stay where I am for now.

Yours, Emily

Concord

January, 1864

Emily,

Dear girl, are you hallucinating? Me thinks you are imbibing the sweet Indian drug that Emerson says poets use to "add this extraordinary power to their natural powers."

That must be why you are dilating your pupils and floating on air, while Mr. Higginson waves and buoys you.

Keep it up and it will give you the courage of a hero, the eloquence of a poet and the ardor of an Italian.

To herbs and dreams,

Lu

Concord

February, 1864

Dear Emily,

I have a plummy idea.

I have received a request from a Mr. Storrs, D.D. for a sketch for his little paper "The Drumbeat," which will be printed this month and next during the Brooklyn Sanitary Fair on Long Island. I have already sent off my story called "The Hospital Lamp."

Mr. Storrs seems like a very gentlemanly D. D. Why don't you send him one or two of your poems, anonymously? They will get an airing and see how they fly outside of your little cage. I understand that Mr. Storrs has some connection with Amherst College. I am sure Austin can tell you if he is safe.

Send something about nature, or the war, not one of those poems that leaves the reader on the edge of the cliff about to slide off into oblivion. The people at the sanitary fairs are practical sorts, like me, and will be scratching their heads if you puzzle them with one of your cutting observations swathed in rhyme and rhythm.

Mr. Storrs will be sending me all of the papers so I will be looking for you and yours.

I am as ever yrs,

Louisa

Boston
March, 1864

Dear Emily,

I am sending you the latest edition of "The Drumbeat" with a lovely surprise.

That's your poem on page 7, isn't it? I recognize your words and spirit but not the punctuation. They tidied it up for you, didn't they? Believe me, though I allow my work to be chopped and changed, I did not think yours would suffer the same fate.

Even more surprising, across the spreadsheet on page 6 is a reprint of one of my episodes from "Hospital Sketches." I had no idea it would be reprinted and wonder if Mr. Redpath, my publisher, has given permission.

No matter that we are both shortchanged our due respect, we are published together and will forever be in communion across the printed page. I like our clandestine literary sisterhood.

We must finally meet each other, don't you think? I don't imagine I should come to Amherst now that the "Hospital Sketches" have thrust me into an outer halo of the limelight. Nor could you visit Concord, where the local vigilance committee monitors my every move now. Do you ever come to Boston? We should be able to cover our tracks in this dusty town. Let's hatch a plan.

Covertly,
Louisa

April, 1864

Dear Louisa,

I will be seeing a Boston eye physician and staying with my cousins in Cambridgeport for some months. If the doctor approves and I can find the courage, you can see me there.

Fondly,
Emily

Concord
May, 1864

Dear Emily,

My father wishes to take me to the Fraternity Festival in Boston on June 3. It seems that he wants his dignified friends to shake the hand of his somewhat literary daughter, though I feel more like Cinderella than Cervantes.

I will come to see you that afternoon.

Maybe if I hear you read your poetry aloud I will begin to understand the metaphysics, and if you see my awkward limbs and my tousled shorn head and my nervous energy you will understand my unruly spirit.

May I say I long for Friday next?

Your friend,
Louisa

Cambridgeport
June 2, 1864

Dear Louisa,

I cannot see you tomorrow for truly I cannot see.
My eyes are bandaged and the doctor forbids even the curtains to be opened.

This letter is written by the hand of my little cousin Frances. My cousins will keep our secret faithfully though they are agog that I know a real lady author.

I regret the delay in our acquaintance,

Emily

Concord

July, 1864

Dear Emily,

I've been wild to hear if your treatments go well. I know you are being careful & do as the doctor tells you. With luck, your bandages are removed already. Don't resemble Homer and Milton too much, dear, and let me know as soon as you are well enough for a visitor.

That Fraternity Festival which I attended after you jilted me was thrilling and ridiculous. I was trotted out with the great ones and made to nod and shake hands with people who wanted to meet the revered authoress of "Hospital Sketches." One deluded lady pined to be introduced to me saying "Mr. Alcott is a great man, but his daughter Louisa is greater." It takes very little fire to make a great deal of smoke nowadays. I liked the experience, but worry that I will start to think what they say is true. I needed to scurry home and get back to work and try my hardest to do more, do better, and deserve the glory.

I miss your letters, but know you are forbidden to write. Do nothing to lengthen your convalescence. If you need me, send to

Your Lu

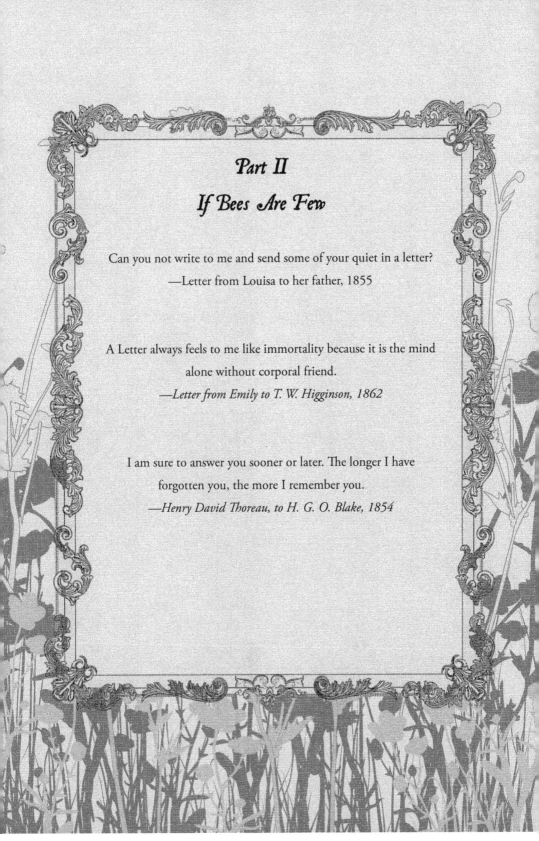

Part II

If Bees Are Few

Can you not write to me and send some of your quiet in a letter?
—Letter from Louisa to her father, 1855

A Letter always feels to me like immortality because it is the mind
alone without corporal friend.
—*Letter from Emily to T. W. Higginson, 1862*

I am sure to answer you sooner or later. The longer I have
forgotten you, the more I remember you.
—*Henry David Thoreau, to H. G. O. Blake, 1854*

Concord
July, 1865

Dear Miss Emily,

I hope that my dear pen-friend has not forgotten me.
Being a sensitive soul, perhaps you refrain from writing in order not to condemn the travesty of my novel, which you may have heard caused a very small commotion. My <u>Moods</u> appeared to the public in a shape I hardly recognized myself, no wonder there was confusion about its motives. I worked on that book, on and off, for over five years and wrote as true as I know how. I will defend Sylvia and her whims and passions, for she was trapped in a marriage which seemed like a burden and neither man could help her right the wrong.

Here I am emoting as if you have even read my blunders! No matter, I write to you with better news. I plan to become a bee again and set out to further fields! I am packing my trunks full of daydreams and schemes and heading across the ocean to Europe. It won't be the free and wild trip I have longed for — money is my obstacle — I go as a companion to an invalid and will use my nursing skills to pay my fare. We sail this week from Boston to Liverpool.

Think of it, Em, Dickens' London and Goethe's Rhine — I shall fill my senses to the brim with the old sights and my mind with the latest thoughts and try as much as I can to explain it later, in my stories. My heroines and my scenes will be full of French fashion and allure, crumbling turrets and wily gamins. It ain't Concord or Amherst! Wish me luck — —

Good bye to all this
Yours,
Louisa

Vevey
November, 1865

Dear Emily,

We have been on such a pilgrimage for the past three months that I only now have the peace and presence of mind to send you a few thoughts about my own personal Grand Tour.
My charge is gaining strength, enough for her tiresome brother to leave us to recuperate quietly on the lake in Vevey, while he travels on to Paris. This suits me well as we have struggled through England, France and Germany and have earned our respite. I will not repeat for you the list of sights we attained — you can refer to your Baedecker for that — but will try to give you an idea of what it really <u>feels</u> like to be here. (Still, I would not be a very useful bee if I did not tickle you with the visions of two days on the Rhine, which left me richer and better for the memories, or of Coblenz with its view of the fortress, the moonlight and the bridge of boats, or hearing the tread of boots echoing as troops crossed it! — and yet one more sight: Goethe's House, in Frankfurt, a tall plain building but for its Dutch roofline.)

The nations I have visited are essentially different from our urgent, always doing and changing Yankee existence. The English countryside is as placid and gentle as a nursery. In France, politeness is such a national trait that the poorest workman lifts his cap in passing a lady, while the Emperor returns the salute of his shabbiest subject. I will likely bring home empty trunks, but my head will be full of new and larger ideas, my heart richer in the sympathy that makes the whole world kin.

For this purpose, I like stopping here at Lake Geneva better than moving from place to place. The air is pure, the exercise wholesome and I spend every evening studying the way different nations interact in society. The haughty English dowager with her demure ward barely acknowledges our existence, which is better than the Southern American "gentleman" and his family who declared he will not take dinner with the "Northern devils." Add to this a Russian doctor, Spanish aristocrats, gentle Scottish spinsters and one forlorn Polish soldier.

Ladislas has been my special project. The evening he arrived, he was placed at the end of the dinner table, near the drafty door, and it did not take but a moment for me to note his wan face and thin cough. I spoke to Madame after and the next night changed my place with his. He enjoyed the comfort near the hearth and since then has devoted himself to me. He gladly plays my errand boy and escort, carrying my shawl, collecting the brightest bouquets, struggling with my French and making every day delightful. He has the natural, charming ways that European men employ so easily and that make a woman of any age feel beautiful and fascinating.

Not that I am beginning to think that old Lou could be fascinating to the lad, but I know he needs my attention and care. The boy is sick and I must see to him. One day I smother him with hugs like a proud Mama, the next I nurse him with smelling salts and a good clap on the lungs to set his breathing right, another day I correct his English translation like the good teacher my father would have me be, and nicest of all are the days when we walk together on the wide, low wall, below which lies the lake talking and laughing and helping him to forget his many losses — the death of his comrades, the illness that may claim him, and the irretrievable loss of his first innocent love. I will be mother, nurse, friend, teacher and lover to this war-torn boy, who needs everything a woman can give to be whole again.

In the evening, he seems nearly restored, when he plays the keyboard with vigor and his pale face glows. Later, alone on my balcony, I plan all the lovely things that will crowd my future tales — boats with lovers gently skimming the lake, stone churches with old gray monks in their cloisters, bright peasant girls yodeling as they bring milk from the meadows, sharp haggling in the alleys among the merchants and the housekeepers. But I also dream of daggers and dungeons, mistaken inheritances, and the pitiable way that mothers force their daughters, barely out of childhood, into loveless, mercenary matches — all these stories will sell easily in the gazettes.

Apart from all this, there is the elegant, heartbroken, pale faced soldier in blue who plays passionately on the piano and murmurs little phrases in French (some of them are ridiculous puns, I am told!) — who longs for a friend and hopes and hopes for — something. I don't know what I will make of him, but he will be in my stories, too.

Adieu,
Louisa

Nice

April, 1866

Dear Emily,

We have been quartered at Nice for the last four months, and I have begun to feel that I am indentured here, to serve silently until my sentence is up. I do not want to be ungrateful, for I have seen such luscious landscapes with mountains and palm trees, had a very few escapes to the vineyards, and several glorious walks at the Villa Valrosa, but things are getting tedious here.

Miss Anna continues to expect a cycle of shawls, elixirs, spa treatments and doctor's consultations. On only the finest of days does she consent to ride in the carriage along the Boulevard des Anglais. Then I glimpse the charming scenes I am craving: the sparkling sea, the ornate hotels, the elegant ladies, and the dapper young men. Most especially, I gawk at the fashions, the classic draperies and flounces of the ladies and the ascots and buff kids of the gentlemen. A— rarely consents to a day in the country (too hot), or a day exploring the churches (too damp), or a day walking the Promenade (too tiring).

The doctors have had a challenge to try to find a treatment, and I have begun to think there is no physical malady here. I know for certain there are days when my bones and nerves ache, and I am the more infirm of the two. Because of my height and my sturdy build, A— thinks I am in top form, ready and able to wait on her. That's where my acting skills have served me well, and when I smile at her, though I'm ready to put her eyes out with my knitting needles. I begin to think that she will outlive me.

Marmee has worried enough about me and, bless her, has somehow borrowed money to send me home, via England, my heart's desire. We have friends, the Conways and the Taylors, in London and I am to stay with them before boarding my ship back to the shores of Columbia.

As I am in Nice and sail to England from Le Havre, it is nearly necessary that I spend a fortnight in Paris along the way. Anna clucks at my brazenness in going unaccompanied to sinful Paree. But, I've been on my own, on and off, since my parents sent me to Boston to eke out my fortune (and theirs) at twenty three years old, never questioning my morals or my secrets. My friend Ladislas is there and will be a kind and helpful guide. I feel that the greatest adventure and romance finally lies before me.

Don't write, I will be at no fixed address, until I am home.

Fondly,
Louisa

Amherst

August, 1866

Dear Louisa,

Would that my welcome could be at your side. I would shower you with blossoms and rose petals. You are returned to your quarter. Nothing is awry. The orchards still bear — the river flows — the forest remains silent.

I kept society as I am wont to do — Austin's Sue for a sounding board, and a beacon.

I spent time with Miss Eliot, Mr. Carlyle and Mrs. Browning. They did not like to be put on a shelf as close to Ik Marvel as I dare. I have read again even his slim volumes.

The two chicks across my yard do well, they chirp and scamper and I dote on them anew. This Sue has done for me as well.

I send in this letter an offering of sorts, as I do so sparingly to those few others whom I trust. Ne'er mind the scraps, do not judge my earnestness by the informal dress. The back of envelope holds a thought as well as my gold-lined cards. The paper which wrapped the flour now comes to you risen as with yeast.

Accept these as they are all I own.

Ever,

Emily

Sepal, petal and a thorn

Upon a common summer's morn,

A flash of dew a bee or two,

A breeze

A caper in the trees —

And I'm a rose!

September, 1866

Dear Emily,

Thank you for your latest poems, my heart adores them but my head spins trying to decipher 'em, so I will stop trying. You are either half cracked or a <u>savant</u>, and as I like my friends to be sane, let's both agree you are a genius.

There is a young girl in Concord who attaches herself as an adoring goose to Henry Thoreau's sister Sophia, and sets her up to be the image of womanhood as if being near to greatness is enough. She is a silly young thing, one of the Loomis family, who the Thoreau aunts have protected and harbored for two generations. She moons about town every summer as if the rarified air will make her a genius with each breath. Sophia gave her a set of Henry's homemade pencils for her birthday and she fancies herself a writer. Of course, the august man would have been as impervious to her adulation as an oak tree and as pure and as steady.

If genius could be gotten by keeping the right company, I'd have it for sure. But the great philosophy that emanates from our town has never been clear to me and I can only imagine the heights of thought in the heads of our dear Mr. Emerson, dear departed Mr. Thoreau and the silver-haired Plato of my own hearth.

I abandoned the notion of genius long ago, the inspiration of necessity is all I've had and I only hope that my writing can entertain and sometimes instruct people in a helpful way. When I'm not imagining fancies, well, then I can only report the impressions of my own life, bundled up with a dose of Marmee's good sense and the bits I've gleaned about morals from Parker, Sanborn and that lot. Talent isn't genius, and you can't make it so.

You, on the other hand, seem to soar to the heights of Olympus and fly above our uncomprehending heads with a vision that is not entirely human.

Don't bump your head on the clouds and come down from time to time to send a line to

Your faithful Louisa

Concord
March, 1867

Dear Miss Emily,

I lift my pen today but do not know if I will be able to finish even this short note, or spin off into a fit of dyspepsia, pains in my gut and my head, weakness, dizziness and all 'round despair.

I sent off twelve stories in three months at the end of last year, and since January, I sit, blocked, fatigued, exhausted and useless. When I chance to walk in the garden, Mrs. Hawthorne peeks at me through her curtains, stunned by my sullen and wasted frame. When Sanborn meets my father in the evenings, he doffs his hat to me with a soundless nod, and a look so solemn that I run to the mirror to see what he sees — and it is a worn, gaunt visage with dark rings about the eyes.

I've developed an oyster-like objection to being torn from my bed. Done nothing for a month but sit in a dark room & ache, but I am not dead yet.

I suppose exhaustion from overwork slowly fades. I can't stay in this condition for worry about my family weighs upon me. And if I do not flit about, how can I be your bee? This isolation oppresses me as much as the fatigue. I shall drag myself back to health, sooner or later.

With hope,
Louisa

Amherst
April, 1867

My dear Shut-In,

I read your suffering with alarm, and then — exhaled — glad in my ghoulish fashion — we are in this the same.

Pain — does it creep across your soul or come as a thunderbolt — blacken all your vision 'til you see but a sparkle, a scintillation, a crack of light that widens and widens and bursts again throbbing against your skull — aching to get out?

Does it sharpen your senses to a razor's edge — or does a fog settle on your eyes, nose, ears, so that there is naught but haze and mist?

Is the nausea innate — internal — or from the awful smell of decay that presses from without? The stab — inflicted by the doctor's probe, or worse, from within?

Does pain tear bone by bone or insinuate — like a gnawing stiffness, all the little creaking joints — the ones needed to clasp a pen — and so, stifles your words —

But revival comes, after a bout — the words come first, they draw you out — mending, vegetal, apothecaric — narcotic or stimulant — your Senses return and then the glow of sun, more radiant by thrice.

Be well,
Emily

Gamps Garrett
Boston
April, 1868

Dear Emily,

I've been scribbling in my hide-away in Boston and being paid handsomely for my little tales for children, my editor's work at "Merry's Museum," my notes from my travels in Europe, and all the while churning out sensation stories that no one expects come from my pen.

But, all my satisfaction and independence may come to a decided halt this month. My father has got me into a pickle and insists I stop everything and write a book for girls. This wretched book was suggested by the publisher, Mr. Niles. I've been trying to ignore the man. What impertinence! Why not ask my father, the esteemed educator, to write a book for children? Would it be beneath the dignity of a man to do so? And it is just precisely my father's inscrutable writing that has got me into this situation. You see, my Pater has made it impossible for me to say no, for he has gotten Mr. Niles to agree to publish his tedious book of essays if my little novel is thrown into the bargain. And so my father sets it up as my responsibility to the family, whose bills have begun mounting again, and to <u>him</u> because he so wants his own name on a binding, that I must write this infernal book.

I imagine Father with his ethereal air and unending conversation trying to convince Thomas Niles to publish his unreadable essays. I see Mr. Niles tearing his hair, "Enough, enough! I will publish your blasted, wandering, impenetrable manuscript if you get Louisa to write that book for girls!"

<u>A book for girls</u>, as if I know anything about girls today! Boys have always been more my line. I only know what my own sisters and I have done and lived. There is one thing that girls know best of all, and that is

the warmth of home. I will put in your famous brown bread and my apple slump but also the true part of home that inspires our flame and keeps our secrets . . . you know that home Emily, it is your secret treasure. Perhaps my book will be as much about the home as the little women who inhabit it.

And how will I deal with this father of mine who barters my talents and my freedom? I shall make him only a shadow in this book for girls. We Alcott women have had plenty of time to live our lives without him from the very first years of my life. He actually left my mother with the first two toddlers and took a room in Philadelphia where he could study and write without distraction. He went away to England to pursue his dreams when I was eight years old, leaving my mother to shoulder on with no particular income. We pulled together and never cared for a male protector or provider since.

So somehow this book will be about women working together and thriving together. And perhaps about the kind of home that makes strong women . . . the kind of home that women create, that is safe and ennobling and free of domineering men. My men will be in the shadows . . .my boys will be as feminine as my little women will be strong. Let's see if Mr. Niles can publish that!

So wish me luck with this dreary project and do not think the worse of me if I write sentimental rubbish.

                                        Ever,
                                        Louisa

Amherst

December, 1868

Dear Louisa,

Your "Little Women" peal with your own spirit — full of life and bravado — and a daring mix of morals and insurrection. Little Ned crows each night for one more page, and I comply, for you twist each action in two directions, and I see you squirming to hide your intentions. Everything is sublimely cunning.

I find that you are perfectly yourself, and so that is the best. After all these years of letters, you never told as much of your family as in the confessions I find here.

How dare you do it? Won't your Pa be sore?

Ever your admirer,

Emily

P.S. Did a sister commit arson on your stories? Could any sister do so?

Concord

April, 1869

Dear Girl,

I've spent most of this winter feeling poorly, head and bones and nerves all awry. I sent off Part Second of my opus with my arm in a sling and my head wrapped in a bandanna stuffed with chamomile. I must have taxed myself too dearly, working to get my little women tucked away, all married in the stupid style that my readers demanded. I don't know if it was the work or the woe about having to tie them all up in a matrimonial bow that set my rheumatism to aching and my nerves to trembling.

I am getting a bit better now. My family seems so panicked when I am sick, that I need to make an effort to reassure them and have sent off some very silly stories to pay the bills that have already begun accumulating.

Young ladies and their mothers have started to poke about the place, some even daring to ring the bell and ask for my autograph. Last week on the Boston streetcar, a grumpy old woman prodded me with her umbrella and announced, "I say — be you Louiser Alcott?" All turned to me. "Well, I'm glad to see yer." Made me a bit proud and happy, I'll say. Just when one gets to liking this shower of attention, one gets a cold hose turned on for your efforts. Yesterday, a young girl was dragged in by her mother, and sat glumly on the edge of her chair. I hardly had patience to pry her out of her snit, when she burst into tears. "I'm so disappointed!" she sobbed. "I thought you would be beautiful!" Well that knocked me off my pedestal for sure.

It's nice, though, to get the checks from the publisher. I'll keep scribblin' as long as they keep payin'.

Still yer 'umble

Louisa

Amherst
May, 1869

Dear Louisa,

If I could be that fly who buzzes near you and lands, just so on the windowpane, to peek — and listen — then flit nearer to your foes and tickle their ear, and nestle in a tightened curl and startle the cheek, to be slapped away — this I would do for you, but no nearer, no louder than a fly on your wall.

How can you do it? To be picked and pried and digested?

'Tis not fame — 'tis notoriety, and you deserve more — propriety.

Fame is what happens after we leave this realm, the stuff of us that stays behind.

Your Little Women have grown and you should be content. I find their ambitions as my own. To be a dutiful daughter and not to be one who obeys. There's a trick to that, to be a thing yet not known.

Your student,
Emily

Boston
March, 1870

Dear Emily,

Do not think I have forgotten my dear friend.
I was busy polishing off the last of the edits for "An Old-Fashioned Girl" as Roberts Brothers wanted them right away. They heard that I was leaving the country for a jaunt on the Continent and so they got in a dither and rushed the publication. It's lovely to be so much in demand, after years of being so sorely rejected.

I will be away, perhaps a year, perhaps more, in France and lands beyond with May and her friend Alice. We shall rely on our own courage, with no guide but our own good sense, three women unprotected except by our Yankee wit. If I don't write often you will hear about my adventures in the little stories that will be sent to the papers to pay for our journey.

Goodbye, God bless you
Louisa

Amherst
March, 1870

Dear Louisa

I have your note of last week. I ardently wish you Bon Voyage and pray you return safely to your home. I quake at the thought of that great sea which you will cross — the odd people you will meet — the unfamiliar places where you will lay your head.

Travel is a chore for all of the Dickinsons, we do not leave our country, nay we have not traveled farther than our nation's capital. I tremble for you. I have no thoughts of straying, except from my doorstep to the dahlias, which encompasses so much that I am as full of wonder as you may be when you glimpse the Alps. This gentle patch is all I need.

Adieu
Emily

I have some words for you today.

I never saw a moor,
I never saw the sea;
Yet know I how the heather looks,
And what a wave must be.
I never spoke with God
Nor visited in heaven;
Yet certain am I of the spot
As if the chart were given.

Amherst

August, 1870

Dear Louisa,

This letter must fly to you, over ocean, over Alps and find you in those climes — as an avalanche — or if you be in Rome — a terremoto — for such a thing has passed through my very parlor. Colonel Higginson was here.

I thought to play a game with him, to be the withering poetess, to be as white as the lilies I brought him and as fragile.

But he sat with so much humility, yet so much power and brought with him the authority of the world. Rather than fade, I fought against his strength, I spoke louder and more heartily and more harshly than I am wont to do. I had to be shrill, to be pointed, to be clever, to be vigorous — in short, to be courageous in the face of his manly gallantry.

He was the one to deflate in my presence. He was not unknowing, but he did not welcome a communion — he pushed against it so as to protect his sphere.

He looked about for an escape. He said he would return, but it will be a long time, or never.

Emilie

Rome, Piazza Barbarini
November, 1870

Dear Emily,

It's not that I have been carousing with counts and barons, nor engrossed in antiquities, & May has held me back from rushing to Prussia to help solve their little war, so my only excuse for not writing is my fits of the doldrums and my ever encroaching demons.

It does not help that ever since I have been in Rome there has been nothing but soggy rain, except that now and then we have flurries of snow, also thunder, likewise hurricanes, the tramontana, the sirocco, or an earthquake. All these calamities arouse the deepest fear and superstition in the occupants of this city, and they either cross themselves and fall helplessly to their knees or shake their fists at the Pope and then plead with the King for succor, rather than leaning to and actually doing something to improve their lot.

I am beginning to get as lazy as the rest of the citizens of Rome and hardly have the energy to whisk the flies from my balding pate on humid days in the flat. All of this ancient city is a big humbug, and I would be glad to shake the dust of it from my sandals, except there is nothing but mud and slime and I have not taken my army boots off once yet. May, as all the truly selfish, sees none of my discomfort and intends for us to stay several months while she laps up the culture and art. I cannot be impressed by a Dying Gladiator who has been gasping for centuries in immortal marble. I saw Raphael's marriage last week and found it stiff and stupid. How I long for dear, pious simple old Fra Angelico, who suits me better.

On one of our last days in Florence, I spent time with the cloistered, beatific old Fra and found one of the only spots in Italy that is not covered with lapis or gold or marble. The dormitory of San Marco has small cells, each one with simple ornamentation, and what peace and sincerity reigns there! You would be in your element alone in a white cell with perhaps only a sliver of the cloister out your portal and a gentle angel strumming a harp painted aloft on the wall. In the refectory of the monastery, I was prepared to view the thousandth "Last Supper" with all eyes raised to heaven and a silly expression on the Savior's face, when I beheld an amazing pictorial rendition of my serene father's motto "The Lord will provide." There, across the far wall, hovering above where the monks took their meal, St. Dominic prays while two flowing angels answer the petition, their arms laden with loaves of hearty country bread. Now if that's not a simple, practical lesson, I don't know what is.

I have been honored by Mr. George Healy, the great portraitist of our American presidents, with a likeness of myself. Really, I am dumbstruck by his interest. Looking at the painting is like looking into a vision of my sufferings. He tried very hard to make me seem alive and thoughtful, but I wonder that no one else sees the flushed cheeks, the tearing, sunken, dilated eyes and the haggard cheeks due to my loss of teeth. I am old before my time, more due to the opium I take than to the rheumatism I suffer. On the days he asked me to sit, I was refraining from my dosage, in order not to look too dreamy or exotic. This is the drill here: my aches and arthralgias gradually get so bad that I begin increasing my dose of laudanum. I get some rest and relief and then start the dismal process of trying to refrain from the accursed crutch. You cannot know how hard a thing it is to give up when I need it so much. If I excuse myself from meals or soirées, May and Alice think that I have been upset by one of the messes the cook prepares here. I spend days with cramps, retching, and am relegated to eating only polenta for a few days. They only see the flush of rheumatism and the neuroasthenia of dyspepsia. No one guesses the rigors of opium withdrawal. Be glad you never touched the stuff, even back a decade ago when you were moiling and boiling those thousands of poems and raving through those unmailed letters.

May is content seeing me scratch away here. I am working on my dispatch "Shawl Straps" or gathering notes for another short story, anything to make the payment on next month's rent and wine. All my labors keep her in finery and grant her lessons with the masters here. She thinks I am repaid by her presence.

Colonel Higginson came to you! I cannot picture it. I can see him in an Army tent, surrounded by muck and men. I can see him in the lecture hall, arousing passions against some injustice. I can see him at the side of his dear wife, gentle, expectant, caring. But I guess he <u>would</u> bolt at your convolutions, thinking you half mad, I'm sure! Send him a poem about himself and he will mistake you completely.

Perhaps I am in too foul a mood. When I am not wet, or cranky, or aching from my disease or my withdrawal, I <u>am</u> glad to have seen this classical cesspool. Though Rome has not been all I expected, the Italian lakes and the Alps and the gentle countryside of Tuscany were as balm to my soul. "Dolce far niente" is the drill here and it does not fit this New England maiden.

To Boston and Emerson,
Louisa

P.S. I am using your sister's name as my character in the "Shawl Straps" escapades. Lavinia-Louisa is only thinly veiled.

Rome

January, 1871

Dear Emily,

I am still stuck in Rome, and the gray, wet weather matches my melancholy spirits. You may have read in the papers — as I did — that my beloved brother-in-law John died suddenly last month. We had not heard before I saw it in the journal. I pity poor Nan being alone to grieve without her two sisters nearby. Their little love story was calm but true, so much like two turtledoves were they, for the ten sweet years they had together.

Their marriage taught me that it seems useless to hold out for a God or hero, when one should be contented with good men, who may lead prosaic lives, wear unfashionable clothes and whose main accomplishment seems to be keeping their temper. John's dear, quiet, steadfast, devoted ways opened my eyes to the powerful duty that men embrace when they say "I do" and promise to protect and provide for a family. He never knew that our friend Alf shared a letter that John once sent him. Listen to this sad, stifled cry, "A bookkeeper goes into the treadmill every day at a certain time and comes out at a certain hour … I go round and round in the one beaten track… Don't, I pray you Alf, allow yourself to get into the treadmill." There is nothing more noble than this, that he carried his burden with courage and endurance, with true self-denial and a real element of cheerfulness.

Since I heard the news I have determined to work in the only way I know how, and have begun scribbling a story in order to provide for Nan and the two dear babies. I cannot make up the loss to my sister and the boys, but I will try to be breadwinner, spouse, father, and consoler to them. I had begun to think that my heavy duties were over, that Mother and Father and May were cared for and comfortable. Now, I have three more mouths to feed, backs to clothe and bodies to warm. I will be the beast of burden to provide for my powerless loved ones. Though I am not on the same treadmill that John trod, and I thank the Great Provider for my skills and success, something like despair does come over me when I think of spending the rest of my life in that quiet house, devoted to humdrum cares, and the duty that never seems to grow any easier.

I wish I could have your peaceful type of contentment, finding comfort in each day and joy in the prosaic details of life. I am miserable with worry while I am away from Mother and Anna, and miserable with the thought of being their support forever. Does your role as dutiful daughter really fulfill you more than writing splendid work or seeing the world? This colt is headed home to tug in harness, but I may need your kind whispers in my ear to keep from bolting.

Ever yrs,
Louisa

Amherst
March, 1871

Dear Louisa,

And so I whisper to you "Come home, Bee, Come home." You may find it not so tedious as you fear — for Home is where each soul longs to rest — here is what I know.

You will remember — years ago — when I was sent to the doctors in Boston — the carriage drew me away from home, though my eyes strained to retain the spot — once that faded I focused instead on the church steeple — which fell in time — I felt the immeasurable pull of the stars drawing me into their orbits, the stellar arc so vast, so immense that I became insignificant, incalculably small, away from home.

That same arc that made me shudder you must now entrust to navigate you home. Oh Lou, if you could see the ship that will bear you back — as I can see it from the vista of the heavens — a mere spot in a raging sea — until it nears and begins to loom and only gains presence again near home.

We are like two celestial bodies, your orbit far flung and mine tightly rotating — but gravity balances our ellipses — and keeps our worlds intact.

Come home, and you may find that home is all you need.

Em

Boston
October, 1872

Dear Emily,

Don't know if you've been writing. I am in Boston. I couldn't work at home. Mother's needs, Father's flights, the door rings and it is always a distraction.

I need new ideas, too, for I have been asked to concoct another serial, and intend to write about the opportunities a woman has for advancement. I was calling it "Success" but now have changed it to "Work," for we may work for another fifty years to fight out of this cage and see if then we can claim our experiment a success! I say let woman do whatever she can do — remove the impediments — bring on the opportunities — only let me do what I can do and no more, but certainly no less!

I am not a "rampant women's rights reformer" but every man and woman is made equal, every man and woman should be educated, every man and woman should have the vote.

My friend Lucy Stone has taken over the reins of "The Woman's Journal" and I intend to report at times for her, and urge women in any way I can to get involved. She has her offices open to an engaging group of women every week, and we chat and support each other and plan our approach. This new sorority is what I needed to get my engine steaming!

I am writing Lucy Stone a little poem, the start is below.

No Surrender,
Louisa

Ho! All ye nervous women folk,
Who sigh that you were born,

Come, try a sovereign remedy
For half the ills you mourn.
I lately have discovered it,
And proved its potency,
By tasting at the fountainhead —
Tremont Place, Number Three.

Amherst

November, 1872

My dear girl,

I s it "seacaptains" we are after?

    I prefer not . . . as "dear Emilie" — daughter and sister — I have no agency.

My Bible tells me so. One reads the Bible as suggestion — a chart — the words are weighted but by no means inviolate.

    But if I be an earl or duke then I rule over my province.

    My subjects are words — the dominion is poesy. Is there suffrage there?

                    Ever,

                    Emily

My Reward for Being, was This.

My premium — My Bliss —

An Admiralty, less —

A Sceptre — penniless —

And Realms — just Dross —

When Thrones accost my Hands —

With "Me, Miss, Me" —

I'll unroll Thee —

Dominions dowerless — beside this Grace —

Election — Vote —

The Ballots of Eternity, will show just that.

Newport, Rhode Island
January, 1873

Dear Emily,

I have just spent a frivolous week in Newport. A ridiculous place where the richest have mansions built one on top of the other in order to huddle near the sea, where balls, and teas and cotillions take the place of real industry and where your hero Colonel Higginson has his little cadre of female writers, who seem to bend to his every suggestion.

There, I've said it. I do not understand how you continue to value his criticisms. He is shaping the opinion of editors as to what is proper and good taste in poetry, and by so doing turns them against your style of writing, while merely advocating for his own. Meanwhile, his little coterie of clingers and his harem of hangers-on clamor to imitate his style. What more can we expect from a man who has said, "It is no discredit to Walt Whitman that he wrote Leaves of Grass, only that he did not burn it afterward."

And worst of all, I have heard from Helen H. that he has shared your poetry not only with her, but with more of the group, Kate Field and the Woolsey sisters and they read not simply your poems — but know about your letters and mock and parody them in a whimsical style. Emily, you are being betrayed by Higginson and I could not say a word lest I break my promise to you to keep our friendship unknown.

I thought it best to tell you.

You need not defer to him. Keep your poems as breathless and sacred as they are. I will always value Colonel Higginson's service to our country and our righteous cause, but I have cured myself of the delusion that his literary opinion is important.

Forgive me,
Louisa

Amherst
February, 1873

Dear Louisa,

N o pardon is given for no offense was made.
I do not seek him as a sage — but he is useful to me still.
He guides me as to what is the current. He has pointed like a
compass toward safety.

I cannot say ne'er mind for — it grieves to be mistaken—

As it must grieve the loon to have its note always called mournful and
the spider her work to be swept away each morn.

I knew the essence if not the full before 'twere told — but still I thank
you for your constancy, friend.

Emily

P.S. Perhaps the whole United States should laugh at me, but what of that?

I reason, Earth is short —
And Anguish — absolute —
And many hurt,
But, what of that?

I reason, we could die
The best Vitality
Cannot excel Decay,
But, what of that?

I reason that in Heaven —
Somehow, it will be even —
Some new Equation given —
But, what of that?

Amherst
June, 1874

Dear Louisa,

We have buried our Father.
We could not have known that such a solid pillar of prose, of all that is real and out there would be the first to disappear.

He was without us, alone, afar. I wish he did not know he was leaving us — it would be a frightful thought — and if he had not time to query God 'tis well enough — his militant, rigid prayer might grate on angelic ears —

Yet for him, trumpets must sound!

They echo still in my brain.

Emily

To know how he suffered would be dear,
To know if any human eyes were near
To whom he could entrust his wavering gaze
Until it settled firm on Paradise.

Boston

December, 1874

Sweet Em,

I have not heard from you since you wrote me about your father's death but I have no doubt that your words and thoughts have not been silenced by this affliction. I have found that as Time makes the burden bearable, our loved one can seem almost closer, with a spiritual kind of sweetness that seems true. Have you felt this yet? If you have not, then throw yourself into your work. Throw yourself into the scrubbing or sweeping with all your might — it gives one the courage to continue on without grumbling. Put yourself to your pudding as much as your poetry, and get some relief with anything which occupies your heart and soul.

I know, too, that you are well because I have had many thoughts of you these six months. All those thoughts tumbled up into a scheme to put you into my next story for girls which should be rattling the brains of young ladies shortly. Never fear! I <u>know</u> your shyness and your wish to withdraw from the world. No one will ever recognize you, but <u>you and I</u> will know the joke, for I've sprinkled you through the pages for my own sanity. While I deliver this pap let me at least honor my friend who has always brought me back to purity and truth.

First, there is Aunt Peace. With her pastel wardrobe, her serene air, and keeping of confidences, she is you as I picture you, cherishing your young-uns across the path, being the simple, honest and quiet counselor.

Then, there is a lad in the story, Mac, the bookworm and "weakling" of the cousins, who must "man up" and face a terrible affliction to his eyes. He needs to stay indoors, away from the sunlight, and is laid up for a year. <u>His</u> sacrifice and worry is <u>yours</u>, your eyes, your condition and your self-imprisonment, never asking for sympathy, but resigned and accepting.

And last of all, though the character is not a bit like you, there is a young servant who "sang like a bird and worked like a woman." I hear you in my thoughts expounding your rhymes and poetry as you race around the house sudsing, beating, baking, your sweet voice singing all about the place.

So, when I have my next blast of fame and honor, as your Amherst neighbors devour the pages of my latest child, never will they guess that the jolly and practical Miss Alcott and their frightened and peculiar townswoman Miss Dickinson are the best of friends!

Oh, Em, how I wish you could know public approval! While you, like Goethe, have been putting your joys and sorrows into poems, I turn my adventures into bread and butter. If I could, I would gladly give you all the fame and keep the spondulix for myself. How I wish you would come out into the world with me — out into the sunshine, blinking and staring!

In the meantime please send me some word that you are safe.

Yours ever,

Lu

Amherst

June, 1875

Dear Friend,

Send me, kind nurse, your remedy for a Mind broken — a torpid Soul. My mother lies paralyzed in Body, mute of Words.

A stroke has thrown her on the care of Vinnie and me — we offer some comfort.

She seems in no pain. She never lived much in the world of thoughts, but often relished the role of invalid — now so defined she will be.

One is frightened of the prospect — a long life seems — tedious

— extraneous

Send me some of your strength,

Emily

Concord
July, 1875

Dear Emily,

What a care to watch your mother dwindle down to something unknowable. Your gentle ways and quiet are what she needs right now. Read to her, or make some music. Healthy food is required and not too much meat, it will get her humors agitated and after a stroke one need remain calm. Keep the windows open & the fire low.

My dear Marmee becomes feebler as well, but remains aware of our successes.

She dotes on my work still, relishes a new series just as in the early days when a verse or short story hidden in a "one bit" journal gave her a great deal of pride. She reads triumphantly of our progress, collecting all the reviews in a scrapbook and rereading the letters that come. And if that were the extent of the public's accolades it would be well.

But, last month, a hundred strangers approached the house and presented their "good wishes" and many stayed to tea and others stayed far longer. My Marmee becomes quite exhausted, for much of the time I am off to Boston, or out the back door at the first sign of a clamor at the front. Anna and Marmee bear the burden, and they are kind but becoming bored by the parade.

If you need me, I would come to give you a helping hand, my nursing skills have helped at times. I own a travel chest of medicinals that are sure to marvel you, sideshow not included. In your home, perhaps I could learn to hide as perfectly as you have. Perhaps my public could be turned away.

Louisa

Amherst

October, 1875

Dear Louisa,

I write to you today for your grasp — or your courage —
If one has written, then released words to another — who owns the oration — the donor or the beneficiary?

I mean words of a personal nature, you understand —

I sense I may have been wrong to send my poems to others who might share them — to those I have not acknowledged nor would address —

My cousins tell me this has occurred. The poems I sent to Colonel Higginson were read to a gathering of women last week in Boston. He did not reveal their origin, but the girls knew my voice — They tell me he was most attentive to his recitation — read respectfully and with some comprehension. They tell me the ladies' response was warm — which is of no consequence to me —

I have not sent my words to strangers — often — they fall on unprepared soil and wither—

Spoken without my presence, they seem violated.

Ever,

Emily

New York

November, 1875

Dear Emily,

On your last point, I have always diverged from you. Once I get my tales out on paper, I want them to fly, to the publisher, to the papers, to the hearts and minds of readers.

I never expect that the public will understand my motives. What I find dull gets accolades, while my favorite book took all the knocks. I can't worry about the public's taste, but as it is so contrary, I must make hay while the sun shines.

It's a great pleasure to be in New York, with all the doors I care to open gaping wide for me just because I have written a successful book or two by accident.

From Higginson, who tries to comprehend, it's a compliment, Emily.

Lou

New York

January, 1876

Dear Emily,

You would not approve of how your old friend has been spending the winter. I have been out of my element, spending time with the thinkers and shakers in New York, and yet, it is curious how they make their mark here. Instead of being the writers and the philosophers, the builders and the inventors, they talk about who they think is worthy of their attention and they publish work that they think the country should read and they finance those whose ideas they endorse.

Though I adore the theater and the lectures, the society is abominable. It is all fast money and the latest invitation and one hand washing the other. I have been placed on a level with Joachim Miller, who has made eyes at me at a respectable salon. There seems to be no depth to the waters here and no ethical moorings. My little ship is without a compass and I don't find the safe harbor I require.

Just outside the door of the most fashionable restaurant are newsboys, tramping in the cold all afternoon, while, at the Ladies' social club, the Irish lasses who wait on the high and mighty, leave on streetcars to boardinghouses with only yesterday's potato pie for dinner. There are good people trying to help, but so much more that needs to be done while the wealthy ignore the masses.

My Puritans roots, fertilized with transcendental sentiment, would never sprout in this soil and you, Emily, with your musings on eternity and unsettling visions of the soul, well, they would shrug and move on. My happy children and your roiling rhymes must make a sorry showing in this busy metropolis.

I need to come home to New England and get back to my little moral tales. It's a wonder anyone reads them, if the new world is like this.

Ever,

L. M. A.

Concord

October, 1876

Dear Emily,

One of my favorite townswomen has passed away, Miss Sophia
Thoreau, Henry's worthy sister.

Miss Sophia was one of the staunch women who shook
this town early on and rattled the cages to call others to the cause of
abolitionism. She and my mother — and others — sounded the alarm
and championed John Brown before any of the men had woken up to the
cause. She sent me her rose the day John Brown died, and it was the same
one I wrote my little poem about. She was a fine lady. I am sending you the
clipping of her obituary, and see my marking, "To meet one of the Thoreaus
was not the same as to encounter any other person who might happen
across your path."

I will never get over the impact that Henry had on me. Perhaps he was
the only man I ever knew — ever met, instead of imagined — who could
fulfill every article I required in a perfect partner. He is the rugged hero in
all my romances, the spontaneous genius of the woods, as strong yet solitary
as a bear, as gentle as a water lily, writing with a kind of indelible ink which
grows clearer with time. I am fuming that Sophia left his books to her little
friend Mabel Loomis. The Thoreaus have known this girl since her birth
here, and she spends summers with the family. I think I have mentioned her
before. She pines to be a writer but I doubt she would know a good piece of
writing without someone else's recommendation. Sophia has been altogether
too kind to her and I am left out again. I suppose Sophia knows that my
father's library is stocked with the same first editions of Emerson, etc. ...
but it does smart to have a thoughtless female take away the last items of
Henry's collection.

This girl reminds me of my sister May, getting all the attention and the luck just for the asking. Meanwhile, you and I trudge along, working steadily and wondering when our reward will come.

I know I should feel satisfied and grateful with my success, but my reward now would be some peace, as yours would be some audience.

I am as ever affectionately yrs

L. M. A.

Concord

December, 1876

Dear Emily,

Though in the habit of sending gifts to celebrate the season, I enclose a book — no gift, but a warning, an admonition to send up a distress signal, call out the cavalry.

It is called a book for boys, and I bought it for my nephews, but think it best to banish it from the house before it does some damage.

It's by that Mr. Twain, "Tom Sawyer" is the culprit's name.

I could make no sense of the words and my dictionary was no help.

It's filled with fibs and yarns and tall tales and makes "drinkin' and brawlin' and lyin'" out to be great fun. This boy, Tom, doesn't read, and the Bible is for impressing his lady friends.

When I was a boy — I read quite a bit and I knew my psalms and Shakespeare's sonnets, too.

Yours,

Louisa

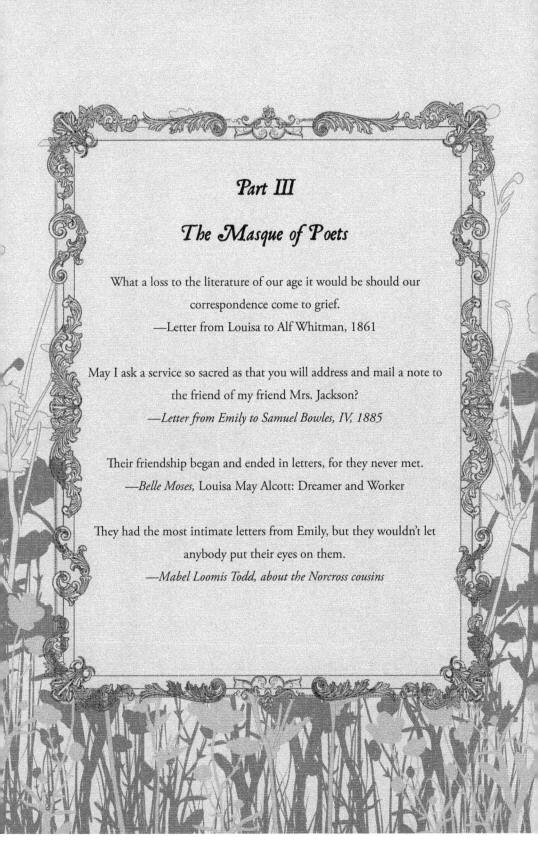

Part III

The Masque of Poets

What a loss to the literature of our age it would be should our
correspondence come to grief.
—Letter from Louisa to Alf Whitman, 1861

May I ask a service so sacred as that you will address and mail a note to
the friend of my friend Mrs. Jackson?
—*Letter from Emily to Samuel Bowles, IV, 1885*

Their friendship began and ended in letters, for they never met.
—*Belle Moses,* Louisa May Alcott: Dreamer and Worker

They had the most intimate letters from Emily, but they wouldn't let
anybody put their eyes on them.
—*Mabel Loomis Todd, about the Norcross cousins*

Concord
October, 1877

Dear Emily,

I am on a death watch with my dear Marmee, slowly drowning in her own water, unable to move, unable to speak at times. I don't know how you have tolerated a half-baked rendition of your mother all these years, Emily. I am angry that my fierce, strong, hardheaded mother is no longer here. Instead, I have a limp, confused, and useless impostor in her body.

There's a dreary, clutching, suffocating heaviness to each day. I watch my mother barely able to breathe, slowly panting her life away. At other moments she seems to have a radiance and be in another place, but then breaks out into a cough or a sweat and her physical suffering is all too real.

On top of my worry about her, I have to chastise myself about my decision not to recall May from Europe. It is too late now, I should have done it sooner, but I went out for optimism, and did not summon her when I should have. I will always have her disappointment and perhaps her wrath as another of my worries. It seems that no one else will be held responsible for the breach: my always blameless father and my compliant sister Anna would not be expected to reach any conclusion on their own. I wonder how I became the man in this family.

I feel that I will be swallowed up in a deep hole when mother goes, for there is no purpose to go on then.

Send me something that I can hold on to.

Very truly,
Louisa

Concord
November, 1877

My dear old friend,

We have just had a Thanksgiving Day like no other, having lost my Mother three days before the feast and buried her three days after. We are in thanks not so much for her release from her burden, but for the lifelong lesson of dutiful acceptance of her trials that taught me so much, indeed, inspired me toward whatever little I have achieved.

No matter her hardships and doubts, her poverty and struggles, she was the mistress of her temper, and the support of her family. Her home was filled with the truest joys of faithfulness, love and, most of all, imagination. When we had the least she created the most, whether it was to whip up a pie or lead us in a magical dance to cheer our spirits and for a moment help us forget how little we had. What others called altruism, she called plain common decency.

I have received a lovely letter from Miss Peabody, who knew my mother through one of our family's great disgraces, the failure of the Temple School. Yes, I will say "our family's" disgrace because I have come to pity my Father, who is so lost and unmoored without his anchor now. Miss Peabody says she "never knew a greater, more tender-hearted, more self-sacrificing human being." What a beautiful epithet for a beautiful woman whose gentle face and mild dark eyes I will always remember as the first face that smiled upon me, the first to encourage and understand.

I am not certain how or why I will go on now. For so long I have been working to make my Mother's last years happy and serene. I was able to provide for her the picture she once asked of me: the Mother in her bonnet, cozily reading her book in a warm and peaceful room, free of concerns, cleared of debt, and released from anxiety. Life is very dark for me now, though I do not wish her back. I shall be glad to follow her.

I think of you and the burden of your mother's infirmity. It is so hard to have them ill and yet so hard to lose them.

Yrs ever,
L. M. Alcott

Amherst

December, 1877

Dear Louisa,

Your mother was a one who added many good and helpful things to our world — who nurtured you, allowed you to wonder and to follow your phantasms. Yours was a special Mother. If anyone was prepared to leave the common lot it was she. I wonder that the Great Creator did not need her to organize His heavens before now.

More than a daughter, you have been her strength in many ways — and how invariably kind and tender you have been to her.

My mother remains uncomplaining, but never close enough to heaven to get there yet.

Vinnie and I do what we can to soothe her way but she stays with us, her tea, her asters, her little patch of sun in the afternoon, it is all she needs. Such a life as this without thought or action — Just existing between the soil and the higher realms, and approximating neither — is a mystery.

Ever,

Emily

Boston

April, 1878

Dear Emily,

I have sent your poem about success to Tommy Niles for his book "A Masque of Poets." Helen Hunt is right — your poems are genius and need to be read. Don't worry, the entire book is anonymous and I sent it with only "From H. H. J." printed in another hand (my sister's) at the bottom and let them make what they will of it. Let them say Emerson wrote it, let them say H. H. convinced you to publish, let T. W. H. take credit for being your mentor, but let us have our little laugh on them.

I will have a poem in the book as well. Remember fifteen years ago when we were published together in "The Drumbeat"? No one knew it then and no one will know our connection now. This will be the bookend of our little joke. I am too stiff and achy to lark in person so let me lark with my mind and my pen. Lord knows I have been behind a mask my whole life. The public does not know half of my work and nothing of yours.

I don't suppose you will thank me — or approve of the punctuation. I let the editors deal with mine and they take out half of my commas and all the dashes but it's all the same to me. Roberts Brothers hates dashes, so be prepared.

Please don't be angry at your busy bee.

I remain yrs,

Louisa

P.S. Niles will send you a copy of the book, try to guess which poem is mine.

Amherst
May, 1878

My dear Advocate,

Some words have been written — some have said, I hear — some have dared to think, I surmise — that my small poem was from the pen of the master, Emerson.

Years ago, before I withdrew, the great mind came to Amherst. I was able to serve the tea at my father's house. He sat near, thoughtful and tactile, safe and sensuous. I wanted to fall on my knees and ask him to be my master. Would he read my poetry? Never, I vowed.

Thank you, friend, for allowing me to achieve such laurels. Thank you, too, for letting them advance no nearer. Never would I have the reach of editors seep through the transom, poke beneath the doorjamb, tap at the flue. I remain safe from scrutiny — from Col. Higginson's disapprobation — from Austin's shake of the head, and the turn of his shoulder, away.

I have found your own words of success "to live, to love, to bless." Believe that you have achieved this too, and take your honest gain. You have wrung from your very nerve and heart, and your success is deserved. Would you could believe it so.

Thank you, worker bee, for the glimpse of infinity. I shall keep my view of the small plot before me and dare not squint into the distance.

Ever your true,
Emily

The lovely flowers embarrass me, they make me regret I am not a bee —

Amherst
Dec. 1878

Dear Louisa,

I dash this off to you before bed, for Vinnie has been in my room, breathless from laughter and describes for me your eminent Sire. She would give you a most vibrant and ideal account, she speaks her mind just as you do, but I will do my best.

She never saw a man so — translucent — from his white mane to his pale blue eyes to his impeccable white shirt. That shirt nearly glowed, she said it just 'bout transfigured him. Who did the washing this week? You have found a good girl, keep her.

He spoke entirely from memory, as if he was addressing a friend in a parlor, yet the Hall was filled to the brimming. Bronson Alcott was never so popular when he was discussing the Emersonian Plan. He seemed bemused by his good fortune. It took all I could to listen to my sister tell me the exploits of your family, as if I did not know that you were tempestuous, forceful and yet devoted to the old codger. That you and your sister have traveled abroad. That your Father was your first and best teacher. He credits his insistence on journal writing as your laboratory, and the start of your success.

Even plodding Vinnie sensed his purity, though. "Not an uppity bone in his body," she said. "Even though he disdained the coffee, and asked for plain water. You could tell he meant it as a compliment to Nature."

How very ethereal he must be. How very consoling, or infuriating, to have such a one run the household. Thank him for making you practical and efficient, as I bless my cold and stern father who prepared me for poesy.

Lovingly,
Emily

Concord
July, 1879

Dear E —

Miss Louisa May Alcott, aged 47, and currently of Main Street Concord, will forever be known as the first woman in the history of that famed classical humbug of a town to register her name as a voter.

Ah, Emily I will no longer be ranked among idiots, felons, and minors but will be eligible to help decide an iota of the future by casting my ballot in the school board election next year. As a property owner, there are 100 women eligible in town. I have formed a Women's Suffrage Society of Concord, and as the chairwoman, I trot about town trying to rouse the women to register. They have come to my home for meetings, a dozen at a time and sit, bewildered and afraid, like the apostles around their Savior and understanding just as little of the mystery being revealed to them. One would think that instead of asking the women to state their own opinion privately on a ballot, that they were being asked to orate an argument in front of the Supreme Court. So far, few have registered, a very poor record for a town which prides itself for its learning and intelligence.

How I wish my mother were here to share in the glory! She petitioned the State of Massachusetts, asking for political rights for women as far back as twenty five years ago. She always said,km "I mean to go to the polls before I die, even if my three daughters have to carry me." And yet, it was she who carried me through those Town Hall doors today, she was with me, otherwise I would not have been so proud.

I enjoyed immensely when the Assessor noted that I had not paid my tax for the year yet and I wrote him a check for the full amount on the spot. He looked so flummoxed — I suspect that he could not believe I possessed the sum, nor that I command it on my own.

Watch me, Emily, I intend to enjoy the rights that God gave me.

Yours for reforms of all kinds,

L. M. A.

Amherst

August, 1879

Dear Louisa,

I have had such a fright that I have been abed with headaches for a fortnight.

July 4 there was a conflagration in our town, I awoke among the clanging of sirens — oil barrels exploding like cannon — and a ruddy bright sun in the midst of night.

I could feel the heat behind my windowpane. The fire would have taken ours, too, had the wind not shifted. I was rooted to my view, I was powerless.

Vinnie came to me and took my hand and told me "It is only the Fourth of July." I had seen, had smelt the fire, but she stroked me and told differently. As if I did not know the difference between the pop of firecrackers and the roar of Armageddon?

I judge I am stronger than my sister sees me. I estimate I am cocooned enough that I would not melt. Vinnie expects I would fracture at the truth. I could not even reprimand her. Was it my place to tell her that she lied? I have not spoken to her about it since. Yet all the town speaks of it and all the papers describe what I know.

I had thought we were in communion but I see now that she prevaricates — and underestimates me.

Yours,

Emily

Concord

January, 1880

Dear Emily,

I never thought I would write these dreadful words to you. My dear sister May is dead. She died just weeks after the birth of her daughter. The child is called Louisa. I cannot tell you how I am still breathing, for that is all I am doing, not eating, not sleeping, not even crying — just breathing, and even that seems to no purpose.

I find no solace in the thought of her soul in heaven. I find no reason for a child to be motherless, for a young man to be ripped from his love and left alone and for me, the adoring sister, to be addled by grief so dense and so dark that I cannot see through it. My grief shall always be double because it is magnified by guilt. I should have gone to her last year, this year, one of the times when she asked me in a half dozen different ways! She wanted me to share her happiness, the beauty in her life, the joy of her love and her art, but I was too chagrined and jealous to rejoice fully with her good fortune. I had a million reasons not to go—my father, my health, my work, my seasickness — how I regret it all now! Emily, if I had been there I know my nursing instincts would have protected her. I would have known the fever was dangerous, I would have called for help sooner — I might have saved her life.

May, so determined yet joyful, so focused yet capricious, so generous yet selfish. She would not be bound by the drab responsibilities required of two aging parents. She devoted herself only to her art, and I thought, only to herself. And while I sent her money to support her studies I did not send her my full blessing. And then she garnered respect from her peers, a loving husband and the ultimate treasure, her own daughter. This was supposed to be my life, a gypsy existence in Europe, an adoring younger husband and all the adventure life could hold. She knew I was green, she knew I only half approved.

But fate would not allow any woman to be so happy, and just at that pinnacle she became a sacrifice to the perfect life. Her reconciliation to me, her sweetest parting gift, was to leave me her dearest treasure, the orphan she leaves behind. I, who had been called the children's friend and America's most eminent writer, now finally have the dearest title that any woman can own: I am someone's Marmee.

I see now why I lived after my world ended once with my Mother's death. I must be here for the dear child, Lulu, and so that Anna will not be alone with father and the three children. I will shoulder on, as I have before. But I do not see that I will ever recover from this loss. I pray that you never suffer such a one.

Understand that I am aching, and I may not write soon, but think of me and remember.

Your old friend,
Louisa

Amherst

February, 1880

My dearest Louisa,

G rief — insinuates as dark smoke from a fire—the hottest fire, from Hades —
        it collects on your tongue tasting like Death —
it enshrouds your eyes allowing no Light —

you reach out — there is nothing at your fingertips —

though you scream there is no Sound —

your ears hear only your own heartbeat — between each beat there is nothing — it seems there will not be anything for a long time — will the next beat come? Or is the heart stopped Forever?

The penumbra of Grief clogs your breath and like a mausoleum, it entombs you, shrieking —

But guilt — that is a yellow thing that comes from within your sickened soul — jaundiced and bilious and fetid.

It is false like vanity and useless as Hope.

Sensibility can never change Fate.

It is God who wills all Things, not ourselves.

Lovingly, Emily

Concord

August, 1880

Dear Emily,

S ometimes, I step inside my home and hear the ghosts conversing, they are in the parlor, as we would be in the evening, together. But when I rush there, they recede to the kitchen, or up the back stairs with a swish of muslin and gauze, as when we held our theatricals.

Anna and the boys are away at the seaside. Father spends day and night with his philosophy students.

I have sent Mrs. Giles, the housekeeper, by steamer to collect Lulu.

So the house would be silent — except for the ghosts.

I busy myself preparing the nursery, and pray anxiously over the white crib with its fancy lace bedding. Do prayers work when they only beg?

My darling will be here within a month and this dejected spinster must be her all in all.

Perhaps it is I who need the prayers.

Ever,

Louisa

Amherst

September, 1880

Dear Louisa,

I have a curious unrest today — a little buzzing — that is more emotion than thought — divined more than understood

I must speak to you — to someone — of one who has come to my aid after my father's death .

My family does not want to hear, for he has ever been a part of it — in my father's study, conversing, debating — or when walking, nearby but less noticed than my straight-backed sire — as in the forest the sturdy undergrowth collects at the foot of the oak — unseen, perhaps, unvalued, until the oak withers — out of the shade they spring up to take its place.

He is not like me — he is all convention and rules — he says the law says this and so you must follow —

He is not like Col. Higginson nor Mr. Bowles who ferment change and groan and bend against what is — for him what is, is to be protected, and those who do not protect it are tried and condemned —

He weighs the evidence wisely and if one ounce, even one drop, tilts the scale then that is the truth to him!

He sees no grays — He has no doubts.

He makes a statement — this is and this is not.

It levels me.

He makes the claim: this transgression is wrong, this man is right, this one — to the dungeons!

But what kindness, what gentleness, no domination, no "lording over."

And he loves me who cannot decide to step outside the door, nor complete my poem for want of scratching out a word for a better one,

who wanders through my own mind, questioning always, so you see — I
acquiesce.

Can life be so — clear
unambiguous —
Could I be a wife?

Emily

P.S. My lord! for the good man's reputation I will not reveal his name.

Concord
November, 1880

Dear Emily,

Y ou describe two beings as different as granite and cambric.
I have seen marriages that are made of such a match. The
heavy one always weighs the other down. I am still searching
for that perfect union of partners. Dear devoted Mrs. Mott, who passed
this week, was perhaps the best of examples. She and her husband worked
together in every fight worth fighting.

You know I'm on the side of Higginson in this respect: Laws, I say
change 'em. No one ever asked me my opinion about the men who make
them, so why am I bound?

And I have all the family I need. The child Lulu has arrived from
Europe. She is plump and blonde, precious, blameless.

Rushed and blessed,
Louisa

P.S. I have never known you to swear and so I think I guess the name.

Amherst
October, 1881

Dear Louisa,

The mountains tell me that it is autumn — such patchwork colors of morn, such lavender shadows in late afternoon! We benefit from the fortune of gold and ruby, garnet and citrine we inherit each year. Should we live in Arabi or Alpine heights, our capital would be different.

A breath of air, a change of season, exactly is what has occurred here —

There is a sweet young woman who makes her acquaintance with my brother and his wife, Miss Mabel Loomis Todd.

Vinnie invited her to our parlor — for a serenade — which I heard through my closed door, though I pried it ajar so she knew I listened. She plays the piano with some grace, and sings with pure tonality. I am told she draws and writes poesy as all young women must these days.

She dotes on her husband, less on her child, and seeks to learn new things. Sue has a plaything on which to concentrate her efforts — for it seems I have failed my dear sister somehow — her disappointment in me is acute, or more likely chronic, lingering, fatal with no cure. Perhaps this new intimate will prove more satisfactory to her needs and her ends.

Sue introduces Mrs. Todd to the town as her especial protégée. There is more gaiety at my brother's house — I hear the tinkle of carriage bells and a soft murmur — his soirées are better attended since the energetic Mrs. Todd has arrived.

I enjoy the quiet laughter that wafts across the lawn — and settle into the corner where my thoughts are.

Yours truly,
Emily

Concord

November, 1881

Dear Emily,

How queer that Miss Mabel Loomis has gravitated into your sphere now. You seem somewhat enchanted by her and I have to give you fair warning. Miss Mabel has been orbiting around the bright stars in Concord, during her summer visits here, since she was a child. She even had the patience to sit and listen to my father (who thinks she is charming) on the old bench under the elm, but mostly hoping that she would be able to spy May ("<u>such</u> a wonderful <u>artist</u>") or myself ("the <u>dear, great</u> Miss Alcott!") as we darted out the back door trying to avoid her.

Mark my words, she will attach herself as an adoring acolyte to someone who she thinks will bring her attention and honor. It could be the President of your University, the most eloquent minister in your community or your well-connected brother. She will swoon like a young girl in their presence and offer their ideas as hers, shamelessly. Lucky for you that you do not go out in society, or you might be the one she tries to grab hold of! So don't be so cozy with her and send her your poems, I wouldn't trust her to know what she's got!

Rather than aspire to be near greatness, I have been enjoying the company of my little cherub. I feel half as old and twice as adored as before she entered our lives. What a lesson to be down on all fours seeing the world again from the perspective of the little ones: their obstacles and their secret places, what charms them and what perplexes, and how a "big person" can be a hero or an ogre! Lulu's questions keep me churning enough ideas for story after story. I have already taken her to the Candy Country and Fairyland and with my other little stories intend to teach her industry, good deeds, humility, and that family will always be her closest bond.

My dear sister May has given me what I have always wanted: a family without the inconvenience of a husband. Remember how I had Christie's husband killed right after the baby was conceived in my long ago novel "Work"? And he was a lovely man, but households run so much better without one, don't you think?

To nurseries and nonsense,
L. M. A.

Amherst
November, 1882

Dear Louisa,

The house is still — our ears strain for the tinkling of the Bell—
it rings in another realm, for Mother.

Vinnie and I are more silent than we knew — the House is
so airy that a draft may catch us unaware.

There is a space to fill. I hazard the Judge to marry me. From what I have
seen of these matters the asker gets to determine the living arrangement.
Can you counsel me on this — 'tis not the convention?

I shall dare do it before he asks, for his Home is where the witches were
and far from my dear plot. Monday he will read of it — if my pen is not
stopped on Sunday —

It would be comfort to have a dear friend after a great sorrow. Many
sorrows, that Sum to desire.

Tell me,
Emily

Boston
November, 1882

Dear Emily,

W hat thoughts we all have as our dear ones leave us! Thoughts, Em, are all I can send.

You reach for an old friend, a devoted friend in your despair, in your hope. I don't think you will find your Mother or your Father, or that thing called family in a new condition. And from what I have seen, it is not the asker but the one with more assets who determines the living arrangement. Guard yours.

You have taken the final walk with your mother, now leave her in the garden she has attained, and see her reflection every day in this earthly one, the flowers the spiritual proof of a goodness in this world, and the rebirth of all living things.

I find it hard to sit serenely in one's soul, with my body becoming a hunched mass of rheumatism and neuralgia. Why this should be remains the question of life, and death it seems. Emily, I know our hearts have not grown old, but our bodies, that is another thing.

In this matter, I can only say your heart will tell you.

Fondly,
Louisa

Concord

January, 1883

Dear Emily,

I have not been able to write as I have been worn, worn in body and mind. My father had a stroke two months ago. He fared better than we could have hoped and is alive. Able to eat when fed, recognize his loved ones, sit in bed and enjoy the pale winter light. What a pity for a man whose life was his mind and his legacy was his conversation! To be able to spout words, but not connect the thoughts, to have the thoughts and then not find the words. I cannot bear to think how long this must be endured. The doctor says his heart is strong, and his constitution fit from the years of healthy living. I may wear out before he does, and this bother and worry will only make me welcome that end when it comes.

Would that I had learned to put aside these cares and live more like my faultless father! When he had little, he learned to eat less and shiver more and felt the pangs all the less because his spirit rose above it all. Elizabeth may have soared with him. Anna followed dutifully without understanding. May was shielded by her innocent age. But Mother and I felt the hunger and the cold and we rebelled against our poverty, and worked to provide.

When I was but ten years old, my mother gave me an engraving of a sick mother and an industrious, caring daughter and wrote, "… I have thought you might be such an industrious good daughter — and that I might be a sick but loving mother, looking to my daughter's labors for my daily bread — ." That was her proof of our bond of love, but more than that our bond of duty and responsibility. What a desperate and isolating act on my mother's part! She had a husband, a brother, a wealthy family, a circle of influential friends, and she turned to a ten year old and saddled me with her destiny. My childhood stopped then. I had no thought but to rid her of her shame and fears and needs. I was provider, counselor and protector. My father stood aside and acquiesced to our dual strength.

Because of my father, I suffered from want as a child and because of my mother, I suffered from wealth as an adult.

Now, though I have wealth, I do not relinquish any of the work to the nurses or the maids. I must do, do, do for my father and the children. No one can do for them like their "Lou Weedy." The more I look, the more I see my mother staring back at me.

Ever,
Lou Weedy

Amherst

October, 1883

Dear Louisa,

H as the sun risen in the east today? I have not looked. Nor know what day it is, except a space without my sweet boy, Gib. Austin's youngest, a child of eight delightful, charmed years — dead for the transgression of splashing in a puddle, coming out wet, muddied and defiled by typhus.

Louisa, I went across the path to see him, but he would not mind a human face nor hear a mortal tone — he heeded voices from another realm, wrestled to find a portal to infinity.

I grew terrified — I clutched the doorframe — the stench of disinfectants, the cloying heat in the room, Austin's somber face, the desperate pawing of his wife at the bedclothes — I went no farther. The way home was harrowing — my homestead was but steps away yet I could not recognize the perspective. I looked at the sky, for the heavens should not vary — but the thought of this poor lad's soul away from here, and where — behind which Star? — stopped me in my tread. When most necessary to know the chart, I could not find a way. I infer Gib's destination was more remote and far more astounding than mine.

Should he now be witness to choirs and clarions, of which I have no knowledge, it would be the welcome he deserves.

Emily

From Blank to Blank —
A Threadless Way
I pushed Mechanic feet —
To stop — or perish — or advance —
Alike indifferent —

Boston

November, 1883

My very dear Emily,

This burden, of all you have borne, is perhaps the heaviest. There is no light behind the cloud of the death of an innocent and sweet child. That he was hale and healthy, and struck down suddenly makes the suffering all the more.

I find no lesson for us in this sacrifice. Rather, it only makes us ache and anger & brings anxiety about each of the ones we love. I look at my Lulu and I think, can I protect her? And from what? God's wrath or His open arms? Are my arms stronger than His?

My words may pierce you rather than console, I am allowing my anger to best me, instead of offering you consolation.

I will begin again.

The memory of all that was sweet and noble in Gib still lives. And so I wish you, instead, to remember his life as a sweet hymn, and on listening, lose your grief and reach for the blessedness that remains.

Let that quiet truth seep into you, for he is at peace, of this I am sure.

Ever,

Louisa

Amherst

April, 1884

Dear Friend,

I have not been well since my recent shock. I have lost another beloved.

 Unable to keep my friend under my own life's key — he has slipped this earth — I can only mourn that I was never more to him but Friend. Had a psalm bound us — he would be closer to me even than a brother. I am no widow but feel a one.

Some days I fall and shake. Darkness, real darkness overcomes me. I am better under covers — who once looked for Sunrise — now craves only sleep. I would sing like the boy in the graveyard — to keep the fears away — but the edge of twilight presses close and I have not the breath to whistle a scant tune, I am silenced. My small plot menaces me, once the quiet proprietor.

The bound fascicles of my life torment me. Locked — as they are — from view.

      Emily

Concord
June, 1884

Dear Emily,

Your last letter was pathetic in many ways. I mourn with you for the loss of your special friend, your poor health, but maybe most of all, for the loss of your quiet contentment. If dear Emily is no longer at home in her paradise what chance have we, the 'umble worms? Ah, Emily, we are getting on in years when regrets are our daily ration. Don't fasten on all we have left behind, all we have lost.

It does not seem your true self to assume the role of widow. I never bemoan my decision not to marry. Sailing my own ship has been my undertaking. With Anna, my dear first mate, Father the chaplain and the boys, who help with trimming the sails, our barque remains seaworthy.

And what of happiness? The only time I laugh and feel truly without care is when I see life through the eyes of my child, or of all youngsters. Yet, I must say it was with some chagrin that I got pegged into that hole of "The Children's Friend." If little people are my legion, I take it as a compliment to my own frankness. As those ancient authors have told us, Jesus once said "Suffer the little children to come unto me etc & etc." There's a reason He spoke to the young. They know hypocrisy, and more, they know truth. I've made things believable and real, or the youngsters would toss my books aside. I've used only my brains and imagination, and been placed in some esteem by society. What I thought was my downfall has been my salvation.

My hard work and ambition have offered me some safe harbor. But still, I do not rest. Never do I assume that we are secure. I maneuver my boat, ready for the next gale. I seek any current to assist our headway.

I have just sold our old house, Apple Slump. It has not been home since Marmee left it. I've unloaded it. With the money, I will rent a fine mansion in Boston and not look back.

Hope and keep busy,
Louisa

Nonquitt

August, 1884

My dear Emily,

I write to you from my new home, with a summer breeze riffling the chintz curtains, and the sound of the sea breaking on the jetty nearby. Lulu and I feel free as the bees — she because she can run and be naughty to her heart's content, with no need to be quiet for her dear old Grandfather's sake, and I because I am free of the curse of a kitchen, as this little summer cottage has no such inconvenience to spoil it. We take our meals at the hotel, or order our tea to be taken on our porch. Now that is luxury!

I take my walks along the seashore, not as solitary as I would like, mind you, as the children flock around me and beg for stories, but I have enough peace to notice that the changes of the tides and the weather here reflect the tempest and tenor of my moods. Sometimes, on the gray, windy days, the ocean swirls and the seagulls fight the wind and I see myself struggling since girlhood against the world, our poverty, my illness, and the general state of injustice all 'round. Other days, when the sea is calm, blue, and lapping gently, I feel the sweetness of life, especially the gentle joy that my little Lulu has brought to my spinster's world. But I like it best here when the whitecaps roll and arch, thundering like stallions on the surf and matching my own headstrong, never ending toil to "make a battering ram of my head" as I said in my youth.

These restful days are just what my poor bones need, and I am thankful for them. As much as I love to look at the sea, I have been a poor sailor, and always cringed in my cabin, pitching and moaning when we crossed to Europe. Yet, I always had a penchant for seeing the world, and if my body had not failed me, I would have been to Fiji, Timbuktoo or Valparaiso instead of sitting by the seashore.

I pity you who have never seen the ocean. I never can figure if it is a failure of nerve or a failure of spirit or just your own arrogance that keeps you so wrapped up in your own world. I will not invite you to see my sea, for I know you will not come. And should you come, I wonder if you would be awed at God's majesty or bereft at His lack of imagination?

Is your view of the ocean grander than mine? I think not, but after all these years, I understand you so little.

Ever,

Louisa

P.S. Your two Norcross cousins have joined the School of Philosophy, now that they are living in Concord. They attend the very gatherings I avoid!

P.P.S. I have changed my mind, I beg you come to the ocean.

Amherst

September, 1884

Dear Louisa,

D on't be cross that I do not, that I never could, come to you. I am happy that the Little Cousins come in my stead. Some days I lose my wits, and fall unknowing, as in a spell — I never roamed and now will not.

You are right that I know only the world I see — rolling hills and drooping orchards and a human village in the distance — snow and stars — a comet — a fairy in the shed, a lizard in the sunshine, the robin at the gate — a sepulchre filled with memories at the border of our worldly limit —

Interior is my habitat. I used to terrify myself about worries of what lay without — the thought of infinity annihilated me. Now the seasons bring comfort — Time is my locale.

You may be right, but if I knew the world more I may have loved it less — knowing it just aslant, 'tis enough.

Emily

P.S. Dan French has a sculpture dedicated in Harvard Yard. When you are in Boston, use your eyes as they would be mine, and see how the young man handles it — does he do a job worthy of the young woman who trained him?

Boston

July, 1885

Dear Emily,

How is it that near a year goes by and we do not write, yet you are wholly with me this entire time? I hope you know how often I think of you. "Emily would never endure this," I squirm at some pompous lecture I have had to swallow, or "Emily would have felt a tremor on this starry night and written an eerie poem about it," because half the time your poetry scares me out of my wits.

When you last wrote, your health was bad. How have the seizures taken you lately? I am ready to go off myself at any time, I tell you, only I am so busy I have no time to die.

While you fain contentment with your little world, you asked me to describe Mr. French's statue. I went to Harvard Yard just specially to please you. I prefer not to be seen at a place of supposed knowledge that still leaves women outside at the gate, looking in, clamoring for admission. Just give her the chance, I say, to try to do what her mind can do.

I am no connoisseur, but the man can sculpt. May saw his talent in the little clay models he built in his father's barn. In John Harvard, he has produced a thinker whose face shows such wisdom that he seems harkening to a vision. How he could put that feeling into bronze, I don't quite know. But, the man is seated, inactive, pondering, with a book on his knee and fancy buckled Puritan shoes, that surely never trod a dusty road. Years ago, I saw a lithograph of "Liberty Enlightening the World" as she would stand in New York harbor. She was powerful, active, clad in Roman sandals and holding a torch to give all the ability to see. This is how I prefer my heroines. Looking at her, one sensed women might be able to get up something for the future. But now she comes packed in crates and disassembled, waiting for the men to fashion her into something in their image. Poor Liberty, still waiting to be made whole. Move over, learned men, sculpting men, governing men. Let the women rule, says I.

All I can do now for my sisters is to write an angry letter now and then. I am too crotchety and too lame to attend the conventions. And Mr. Niles points out that it doesn't help sales if half the population has their nose out of joint.

The said Tommy Niles is pushing me to complete the March family story. It is straining every bit of my nerves. I bet he would be content with receiving some of your poetry. Why don't you send him a neat little portfolio? Is it Higginson who keeps you so cautious? If I listened to the critics, I wouldn't write another word. The more they criticize my slang, the more the public eats it up.

I'd like to be able to say I knew Emily before she was famous.

Yrs,
LMA

Amherst
September, 1885

Dear Louisa,

Your letter amused me — your will suffused the room — a pleasant breeze that ruffled the curtains and sent the cat scampering. After the first burst, it swirled about, unsettling the papers on my desk — then circled the room once more and escaped by the flue. I knew it was gone when my candle flame straightened and flared brighter.

What have I to do with your women at the gates? The chains may rattle, but one has no more power to convert society than to alter the seasons. I welcome your urgency — your Bravery, as always, boosts me and helps me to consider Possibilities.

I have no news of statutes or rights — nor of statues and writing. My only news now are bulletins from Immortality. I am like Mr. French's sculpture — staring into the future — knowing a great secret perhaps — but silent.

You, rooted in this world, so vigorous, so saturated with life — I cannot see you stopping for death — your voice will roar from the beyond and still growl and shake the portcullis.

My seizures are each like little deaths from which I arise — like the phoenix — amazed. My awe is such that I do not accept the permanent state. The arc of heaven can be no more brilliant than the carmine rays before the gloaming.

Really,
Emily

Boston
January, 1886

Dear Emily,

How are you, dear? Are your blackouts better and have you gained any more strength? Are you able to write at all?

I believe we are so very close in spirit that we commiserate with each other bodily. I have been much out of sorts lately, and long for the times when I could work like a steam engine and churn out a novel in three months. Now, Niles is waiting for the infernal end to the March family and the doctor says I can only work a half an hour at a time. If I do more than that, the old top gets muddled and I forget if I've sent the musical boy to Vienna or Leipzig and if the rowdy one ever told Old Aunt Jo about his time in prison.

But it is more than confusion, it is real disgust at the whole way things have turned out for us. I still have May in the story because I cannot bear to break my heart all over again and relive her death. Amy remains a shadow of my artistic girl, for how can I imagine what never <u>could be</u>, what never <u>will be</u> for women in our time? She is followed around by an ineffectual husband who can never protect her from what is her fate. I have also, unfinished, the novel I started about May's glorious artist's life and know I will never pick up that thread.

I sleep poorly, unless I take my laudanum. Then, I sleep deeply, but have such fearful dreams that I struggle to awaken. First, I am pursued by young girls with their autograph books, they turn into creditors waving the monthly bills, and then there is only one figure left, my sister May, waving the letters she wrote to me, asking me to come to her.

Besides the poor sleep, I cannot eat. I have beef broth and milk and that is about all I can stomach. There is a tingling in my mid back, which is part physical and part the sense of dread which I cannot shake. It stays there, always, and I find that I sometimes forget to take a deep breath, as I try to sit so motionless. The dreadful feeling comes to the front, just under my breastbone, and there it mingles with the wretched acid feeling and all hope of appetite is gone. Once my appetite vanishes, my head spins, I feel faint, the vertigo takes over, and the whole cycle starts again. I don't know if it is in my mind or my stomach, this ailment. When I get the tingling in my legs and joints, that I know is the neuralgia from the mercury treatment I was given in the war. That I deal with better, as I know it will not kill me, after all these years. Dr. Wesselhoeft is a dear and bears with all my complaints, convinced that I will get better. He spilled the beans that as he is the nephew of Dr. William Wesselhoeft, he accompanied that grand old doctor on his rounds as a young man, and he knew all the people of any merit in Boston at the time. He blithely gave me a lively list of the politicians and educators he knew, knowing how much I enjoy remembrances of my family's glory days in Boston. His list even included your father and "his family." Seems that Wesslehoefts have kept us both alive, though Lord knows I am ready to welcome the peaceful sleep that awaits me sometime.

Write and tell me how you are, because I worry,

Yours,
Louisa

Boston
March, 1886

Dear Emily,

Never have I sat down to scribble off such a discontented, irksome and woeful note as this no doubt will be. I am all out of sorts <u>again</u> as I thrash about looking for some peace in my mind and on my hearth. All I ask for is some space and freedom to be myself, to write my tales and <u>not</u> to be interrupted by the postman with bills, the nanny with complaints about Lulu and Father with his never ending parade of disciples.

So I shuffle off to Boston and lock myself in an oppressive studio and fire away at my stories. Then, the call comes from home for reinforcements and I decide to pack them all up and take them with me for the winter, where Father can have a decent nurse nearby, Lulu rumble about the nursery, the boys attend a decent school and Nan pore over the fashions and society news. This never suits for very long and spring comes and we shuffle back to Concord, for Lulu needs to gambol in the country, Nan longs for her garden, and I need to get some quiet.

It seems that I carry home <u>with me</u>, all of them wherever I go, but with ten in the house, including the servants, I still find myself longing for that pleasant atmosphere of home-peace that I cherished long ago. I have never found it since the days when my dear philosophical parents smiled on their four daughters, sending the little women out into the world, to the bright, hopeful future. Where have those six gone now? One lost too young to a dwindling death caused by undisciplined philanthropy; a mother, worn by cares and pride to a doddering end; and our sweet summer girl, so ripe on the threshold of her artistic fame, her life's work cut short by the kind of death that only women need bear.

Where five women once supported the needs of our illustrious <u>pater</u>, there remain just two, and Nan worn away to distraction by the moods and melancholy of her restless sister. Home for me was never a place and the home-bodies that made it true no longer exist.

But you, Emily, embrace all the home you need with your two arms and draw it to your sweet breast. Your home is <u>within</u> you, even as you remain within your home. How I long to come to you and lay my aching head and trembling limbs on that breast! Can I come, Em? It seems all the peace and gentleness and friendship I need is there in your welcome. I so need to turn from my cares and loneliness to the household light and warmth and peace waiting to receive me. Our little sisterhood would be complete and our work joined to a greater cause. How our simple conversation would turn divine!

Yours ever,
Loving Lou

Amherst
April, 1886

Dear Lou,

I cannot welcome you to my home—I am on the threshold of the next home.

I am glad that my dear cousins are near you in Concord—they could have no stronger shoulder to lean on—

Either the Darkness alters —
Or something in the sight
Adjusts itself to Midnight —
And Life steps almost straight.

Emily, with love

Boston

May 18, 1886

Dear Lavinia,

F ranny and Lou have sent me the news this very day—and how
like dear Emily to have thought of them in her last days.

Sister, I have been a secret friend of Em, for forever, it seems.
Dear woman, perhaps yours is the only heart that bears a heavier burden
than mine today, for you have lost a sister in blood and I have lost one in
spirit. We both know that sisters are the closest things to our very own
person in this world, bearing with our joys and fears from the very first
day. You, Lavinia, have never been apart from her, together in the same
household all these many years.

I know how hard it is to spare these dear sisters, having lost two, and
how empty the world seems for a long time. May was snatched from us
suddenly at the peak of her joy and I have never recovered from that bitter
grief. But Emily's passing resembles our Lizzie's, who seemed to be so slowly
refined away that the immortal was shining through by the time she left us.
Emily, too, has been one who ever stood on the borderland of the spiritual
world, ready to return to the mystical place from which she came. Didn't
she always say of Heaven that she was "going all along"? Believe me, after
the first sharpness of the loss is over, you will find a sweet & precious tie still
binds you even more tenderly together.

Now the matter at hand.

This packet contains the letters Emily wrote to me. I have found
it prudent to carefully return or destroy any evidence of personal or
sentimental attachments from my papers. Curiosity seekers would love to
have any detail of "Aunt Jo's" life exposed, and not in a kind way. As I am
aware of the depth of privacy and solitude Emily desired, I suggest that

all portions of this intercourse be destroyed, including the letters I sent to her, which you may find in her cupboard. Emily has been clear and firm about her desire to keep her writings private. The gossip lovers, fanatics and general busybodies have tramped over every intimate moment of my life for some time and I could not bear to have Emily handed over to the same sort.

Know that the quiet strength, mastery of words and truly "transcendental" independence of spirit that our dear Emily possessed has pulled me forward more times than she or anyone could know.

When I was most unsure about what success and fame would mean to me, when I wanted creature comfort and recognition and the highest praise from kin and public—when I struggled to "make something of myself"— she sent the following poem to me. It was no coincidence that it is one of the ones Mr. Niles "mysteriously" published without her name.

Success is counted sweetest
By those who ne'er succeed.
To comprehend a nectar
Requires sorest need.

I had the need and then I had the success, but found that having asked for bread, I got a stone—in the shape of a pedestal.

Protect your sister's papers, she chose the truer path.

Yours ever,
L. M. A.

Amherst

June, 1886

My dearest Cousins,

I have received this large packet from a person whose name has startled me and while I think about what to do, you need to keep it safe—and hidden. You will see at once that the letter which accompanied the packet is from the esteemed Miss Louisa May Alcott. She enclosed a collection of letters from our own dear Emily. I daresay you are not as surprised as I am. I discovered only after Emily's death, that although they never met, the two enjoyed a lively correspondence, indeed it seems as true a friendship as Emily ever cherished, for twenty five years.

A word of explanation. Miss Alcott has sent dear Emily's letters to me, as she feared that if found among her belongings, they would become public, and she knows, as do we, that Emily would shudder were that to happen. You know too that I was instructed by Emily to burn her papers, and that I honored this charge only partly. Her letters, in the main, were burned. I say "in the main" because when I came upon Emily's letters from Miss Alcott, I could not bear to set them to flame, I was so stunned that a person so large and so famous would write to our darling recluse. Despite my sister's dearest wish, I feel we must preserve them. You dear girls were devoted to Emily and know Miss Alcott, so you will know best the worth of these letters. 'Tisn't foolish to be prudent, 'tis very wise.

I do not wish for them to be seen, but only to be shielded from the prying eyes of, well, of others I need not name. When Miss Alcott kindly sent me Emily's correspondence, I resolved to send the whole business to you for safekeeping. They are more secure in your home than in ours. I hope to get matters arranged a little in my mind, then I will send you further instructions.

I miss Emily dreadfully and she keeps sending me new surprises. Oh Franny and Lou! You have no idea what else I have found!

Vinnie

EPILOGUE

The academic backlash was predictable. Though the concept of a correspondence between Emily Dickinson and Louisa May Alcott was amusing, even mildly conceivable, the lack of evidence in any journal, biography, or family archival material continued to dissuade the thought leaders. The leading theory was that the letters were a carefully constructed deception, likely an unpublished fiction, by a literary descendant of the Dickinsons, perhaps through the Norcross line.

Did they really believe that someone in the Norcross family had an elaborate plan to perpetrate a hoax, then abandoned the plan? That the letters were forged and hidden generations ago as a literary joke? And that the beauty and immediacy of the words were fictitious? I seethed at the condescension, the lack of insight, the refusal to *see*.

Students and advocates of each author weighed in. Emily Dickinson wouldn't even *like* Louisa May Alcott, some said. Louisa's practical, worldly, energetic stories and her no-nonsense businesslike approach to her craft were the antithesis of Emily's careful and sensitive technique. Louisa May Alcott wouldn't have given Emily Dickinson the time of day, others said. She wasn't a letter writer to begin with, except as it was necessary, and would never have tolerated the reclusive, introspective poet. And yet, there was also a great swell of sentiment that the two dear ladies had enjoyed each other's counsel. Perhaps they had created the work we cherish today because of the insight they gave each other, and the undaunted support they needed to persevere in a man's world. I still maintained that there were too many coincidences in the women's overlapping lives, too many opportunities for their interaction. But because they had kept the communication private, even from their dearest sisters and relatives, and then carefully expunged all evidence from their diaries and papers, the final connection could not be verified. Whether I had slandered their legacy or enriched it was unclear.

I sat at the desk that yielded the lode of beautiful letters, again looking out at the snow. There were no longer any drifts and a few scattered mounds of dark earth revealed the faintest trace of green shoots, surely the earliest sign of the crocus. I sifted through the day's mail. I had come to expect that the sweetest missives came in writing, on floral paper, usually from older readers, who remember a time when sending letters to relatives and friends just a few towns away was part of a young girl's social bond.

I had one of those handwritten, confidential letters today. I could tell from the envelope, which was addressed decoratively, with a daisy and red ladybug emblazoned on the return address label. Inside, there was a letter in beautiful cursive writing and a photocopy of an older correspondence:

June 2020

Dear Miss —— ,

I heard about the letters and want to congratulate you on finding the secret that the old Norcross house held all these years.

I grew up in that very house in Lexington. My parents had bought it from a grandniece, I think, of Emily Dickinson. We were never certain of the connections exactly, but the realtor told us that the house was sup-posed to have a memento, or hidden book, or item of some kind related to Emily. At least that was the gossip. Of course, we scoured the place for any sign of a secret compartment, behind the mantel, the root cellar, the floorboards in the attic. The desk was always our primary target, but we never could find the latch that you were able to open. Once, we pried off the desktop and found an old letter slipped under the green leather. I am sending you a copy. We couldn't tell from this letter exactly what we were looking for: a box, autographs, a diary, but it is all pretty clear now.

There are a few things I know from my eighty years' existence, and some of them are: trust your instincts, don't back down when you are right, and always side with the ladies.

Thank you,
M —— —

Here is the letter she enclosed:

March, 1888

Dear Lou,

Hello dear sister, have you heard the stunning and sad news of Miss A's sudden death? Just two days after her dear old father. And all this time, no one has yet guessed that while we studied at the summer philosophy school, you and I, the silent and studious Norcross sisters, knew of a secret connection between the famous Concord family and our dear, gifted, and misunderstood cousin.

I am most uncertain as to what to do with the items in our safekeeping. Now that Miss A is gone, we need to keep them even more sequestered. We dare not give them back to Lavinia. Have you heard that she took Emily's poems from Sue and gave them to that horrid woman?

We will keep these carefully tucked away until we can see clear to turn them over to safe hands. When and who that will be I cannot see for now.

Take care,
Franny

Franny and Lou, I hope you agree those safe hands were mine.

HISTORICAL PERSPECTIVE

Emily Dickinson (1830–1886), lived her entire life in Amherst, Massachusetts. In the last three decades of her life, she never ventured from her family compound, the Homestead, where she died as a recluse. After her death, over a thousand remarkable poems were discovered by her sister, Lavinia. She is now considered one of the foremost American poets.

Louisa May Alcott (1832–1888), lived in nearly three dozen locations throughout New England, mostly in Concord and Boston, Massachusetts. During her lifetime, she was the most acclaimed American writer of the time, famed for her masterpiece *Little Women*, and the continuing March family series. After her death, her anonymous romance thrillers were discovered. She is considered a beloved children's author, as well as a complex female writer of the post–Civil War period.

In 1862, Emily wrote a letter to the author, social reformer and editor, Thomas Wentworth Higginson, asking him to critique the vitality of her poetry. Why she chose him as her mentor and confidant is one of the great literary mysteries. Higginson was a longtime associate and friend of the Alcott family, dedicated to abolitionism and the social reforms also espoused by Louisa's parents, Bronson and Abigail Alcott. Louisa admired and lionized him as a young woman, and always valued his recognition of her own work.

In 1864, after returning from the warfront where she worked as an Army nurse—which resulted in her first successful book, *Hospital Sketches*—Louisa was asked to contribute a story to *The Drumbeat*, an obscure journal that published just thirteen issues and a bonus issue from February 22 to March 11, 1864, during the Long Island Fair for the Benefit of the U.S. Sanitary Commission. She answered with the story "A Hospital Lamp" in the February 24 edition. Though Emily Dickinson only published ten poems in her lifetime, three of them appeared in the Brooklyn *Drumbeat*, on February 29, March 2, and March 11. In the March 11 issue, a reprint of a chapter of Louisa's *Hospital Sketches*, printed under the heading "A Night in the Hospital," appeared on page 6 across from Emily's "Orchard" on page 7. No biographical information exists about Emily's connection to the Sanitary Commission, or how her poems were submitted to *The Drumbeat*.

Although Emily was a recluse in her family home, she maintained a lively correspondence with many friends and family members. Her favorites were her cousins, Frances and Louisa Norcross, whom she continued to entertain at the Homestead. They were early advocates of her genius and were aware of at least some of her poetry. The Norcross cousins were members of the New England Women's Club, also attended by Louisa May Alcott. In their later years, they lived in Concord and were associated with Bronson Alcott's Concord School of Philosophy.

Another of Emily's beloved correspondents and a lifelong acquaintance was the author Helen Hunt Jackson, who later wrote the novel *Ramona*. Jackson also entered into a mentee relationship with Thomas Wentworth Higginson in 1866, and through Higginson met his literary friends. Ralph Waldo Emerson was one of her admirers. Jackson knew the Alcotts, as evidenced by Louisa's visit to her home in Newport in January 1873 and Jackson's unfulfilled offer to travel to California with May Alcott, Louisa's sister, in spring 1873. Later in life, Alcott and Jackson were considered among the greatest American women authors. Jackson prodded Emily to publish her poetry.

Mabel Loomis was a young girl who was befriended by the Thoreau family of Concord. She spent summers with Sophia Thoreau, Henry David Thoreau's sister. After her marriage, she moved to Amherst as Mabel Loomis Todd. She entered into a torrid love affair with Emily Dickinson's brother, Austin. After Emily's death, it was Mabel, along with Thomas Wentworth Higginson, who edited and published her poetry. She also wrote memoirs about her encounters in Concord with the Alcott family.

Daniel Chester French was the most acclaimed sculptor of the time. He knew the Dickinson family from his boyhood, having lived in Amherst from 1864 to 1866. Emily wrote at least one letter to him, in 1884, congratulating him on one of his sculptures, and the Dickinson Museum, the Homestead, displays one of his works, "The Matchmaking Owls." In 1867 the French family moved to Concord, and it was there, under the influence of Abigail May Alcott, Louisa's sister, that he decided to pursue sculpting. In his own words, written in the introduction to a biography about May Alcott, he says, "Miss Alcott, as the artist of the community ... with her ever-ready enthusiasm, immediately offered to give me her modeling clay and tools ... I still have one of the modeling tools she gave me."[1]

In 1878, Louisa and Emily each had a single anonymous poem published in the book *A Masque of Poets*, which was presented by Louisa's longtime publisher, Thomas Niles of Roberts Brothers.

Several days before Emily died, she wrote her last letter, which was to the Norcross cousins, which simply said, "Called back." Following Emily's instructions, her sister, Lavinia, destroyed all her letters, but could not bring herself to destroy the mass of poetry she discovered.

Personal items of Frances and Louisa Norcross were given to another mutual cousin, Anna Norcross Swett, on their passing. Letters that the Norcross cousins owned could have been in that collection. The final traced descendant of this cousin was Sylvia Swett Viano. who lived in Lexington, Massachusetts.[2] Thus, we have chosen to have the letters discovered in a Norcross desk there.

When Emily died in May 1886, Louisa, a compulsive diarist, wrote nothing in her journal for two months.

---

1   From the Prelude by Daniel Chester French in Caroline Tickner, *May Alcott, A Memoir* (Boston: Little Brown, and Company, 1927).
2   This information is from Martha Ackmann, "'I'm Glad I Finally Surfaced': A Norcross Descendent Remembers Emily Dickinson," *Emily Dickinson Journal* 5, no. 2 (Fall 1996), https://muse.jhu.edu/article/245328.

A year after Emily's death, Louisa's last published book, *A Garland for Girls*, included a story about the relationship between two girls, one a secret poet who had been discovered by her enthusiastic friend. Through the voice of the protagonist, Louisa writes, "Sly thing! To be so bashful and hide her gift!" and "I've tried to write verses myself, but I always get into a muddle, and give it up. This makes me interested in other girls who *can* do it, and I want to help a friend. I'm *sure* she has talent, and I'd so like to give her a lift in some way." In her own sly twist, Louisa names the discoverer Emily, and describes her as a "delicate fern [that] grew in the conservatory among tea-roses and camelias."

Before Louisa's death in 1888, she had systematically purged her journals and letters, destroying anything of a personal or professional nature that could have altered her adoring public's image of "Miss Alcott, the Children's Friend."

No actual correspondence between Emily Dickinson and Louisa May Alcott has ever been found.

Annotations

As the lively little women who adore Miss Alcott always wish to know what *really* happened and what was *made up,* and the scholars and dreamers who favor Miss Dickinson search for explanations of what truly transpired behind her closed doors, we offer these notes.

1861

"this little Rose—nobody knows." Alludes to the poem "Nobody knows this little rose" printed before the date of this letter in the *Springfield Daily Republican*, August 2, 1858. We suggest our readers access the Emily Dickinson poems at www.edickinson.org, where you will be able to read facsimiles of the original poems in Emily's own hand.

"The May-Wine" Printed in the *Springfield Daily Republican*, May 4, 1861. The paper was published by Samuel Bowles III, who was a correspondent and mentor of Emily Dickinson.

"How they hollered and cried" This refers to a real episode when Louisa read her first published story "The Rival Painters" aloud to her sisters, without first revealing herself as the author. Myerson, J., et al., eds. (1989). *The Journals of Louisa May Alcott*. Little, Brown and Company, p. 67. This scene was recreated in *Little Women,* Part 2, Chapter 4 "Literary Lessons." For the complete, original wording of *Little Women,* we recommend Shealy, Daniel, ed. (2013) *Little Women, An Annotated Edition.* The Belknap Press of Harvard University Press.

"The Atlantic takes a poor fellow's tales and keeps 'em years without paying" Louisa wrote these words to her sister Anna in 1860, after her story "A

Modern Cinderella" was accepted. Myerson, J., et al., eds. *The Selected Letters of Louisa May Alcott.* The University Press of Georgia, 1995, 59.

"To make a prairie" This poem was not public during Emily's lifetime.

"It all seems rather queer as the city is filled with rich relations" This sentiment was expressed by Louisa in a letter in 1856. Myerson, et al, eds., *Letters*, p. 20.

"ready to go off like a torpedo at a touch" From Louisa's "A Modern Cinderella," published 1860, said of the character, Di, modeled after Louisa.

"Why are men such icebergs" From a letter of Louisa's mother, Abigail Alcott, in LaPlante, E. *My Heart Is Boundless: The Writings of Abigail May Alcott.* Free Press, 2012, p. 92.

"all that was left him when the dreams fled" and "Even the most kindly thought him a visionary" Louisa wrote these words in *Transcendental Wild Oats* (1873), her gentle farce of the Fruitlands experiment.

"Even we, his family often misjudge and reprove him" Quoted from Martha Saxton's book, attributed to Louisa in her journal of March 1861. Saxton, Martha. *Louisa May Alcott; A Modern Biography.* Farrar, Straus and Giroux, 1995, p. 243.

"perform the coronation-ceremony with his best hat" This little ritual is described in Louisa's "A Modern Cinderella," 1860.

"encourages us to be all in all" Quoted from a letter of Abigail Alcott, LaPlante, p. 112.

"I do think that college men" From "King of Clubs and Queen of Hearts," published in The Monitor 1862.

"Life is my college." From Louisa's journal. March 1859. Myerson, et al., eds. *Journals*, p. 94.

"Striving and learning to be all she can be" From a letter by Abigail Alcott, in LaPlante, p. 160.

"All the philosophy in our house" From Louisa's Journal 1860. Myerson, et al., eds. *Journals,* p. 101.

"politics, cigars and brandy" From Louisa's "Mountain Sketches," 1863.

"equal parts table linen and theology" From *Jo's Boys,* 1886.

"One can discuss Greek philosophy and chop meat" From a letter by Louisa in 1886. Myerson, et al., eds. *Letters*, p. 297.

1862

"Oh! my abominable tongue!" Said by Jo in *Little Women.*

"We do our part alone" Marmee does say this in *Little Women.*

"wonder how many families" From Louisa's adult novel *Moods,* published 1865 and with a revised ending in 1882.

"Some girls are taught" From "The Marble Woman," published 1865 under Louisa's pseudonym, A. M. Barnard.

"homesick for [you] even in heaven" Spoken by Beth in *Little Women.*

"I feel restless" Jo's sentiments in *Little Women*.

"life…is over there" From Emily's poem "I can not live with you."

"There was more yeast" Spoken by Christie in *Work*, first published as a serial in 1872–73.

"Volatility and wretchedness" Words used by Abigail Alcott in describing Louisa. LaPlante, p. 106.

"we must each be what God…" From *Jo's Boys*, 1886.

"I was born with a boy's nature" Paraphrased from a letter of Louisa's in 1860, Myerson, et al., eds. *Letters*, ed. p. 52.

The Massachusetts 27th, Company D was from Amherst. In the Battle of Newbern, March 13, 1862, Frasier Stearns, a close friend of Austin's, was killed.

"Henry used the very invitation" this actual card is filed in Thoreau's Notes on Fruits in the Berg Collection at the New York Public Library.

"I think out sketches of stories" From Stearns, F. *Sketches from Concord and Appledore of 30 Years Ago*. G. P. Putnam's Sons, 1895.

"The way to speak and write" From Emerson's essay "Spiritual Laws." Emerson R. W. *Essays and Poems*. Everyman Library, 1995, p. 76.

"two books half done, nine stories simmering" From a letter by Louisa to her sister Anna, 1860, Myerson, et al., eds. *Letters*, ed. p. 59.

"I had nowhere to turn for employment" This entire episode is true, including the disparaging remark from Mr. Fields.

"It is remarkable what false positions poor women can be forced into" From a sentiment from Louisa's journal entry of February 1862, Myerson, et al., eds. *Journals, p.* 108.

"the mighty magazine has become dreadfully afraid of certain words and ideas" Louisa felt that *The Atlantic* did not publish some of her stories sympathetic to the plight of slaves.

"He never was what ladies call" Words from *The Inheritance*, Louisa's first novel, written when she was seventeen, and discovered many years later in the Houghton Library. Alcott, L.M. Dutton Books, 1997, p. 8.

"knocked down the driver" From a letter by May Alcott to Alf Whitman, in the Houghton Library Alcott archives, May 4, 1860.

"never saw a man dying" Quoted from Canby, H. *Thoreau*. Houghton Mifflin Company, 1939, p. 438.

"wore the worst boots" From "The King of Clubs and the Queen of Hearts," 1862.

"he convinced many" Louisa said something similar in a letter to Sophia Foord, another of her early teachers in Concord, Myerson, et al., eds. *Letters*, ed. p. 74.

"I've always wanted to live in stirring times" Christie's words in Louisa's adult novel *Work*, 1873.

"Action from principle" From Thoreau's "Resistance to Civil Government."

"haunting the hills, the streams" From *"Thoreau's Flute,"* Louisa's poem published in *The Atlantic Monthly*, 1863.

"he is getting up an infantry" Thomas Wentworth Higginson was a captain in the 51ˢᵗ Massachusetts Regiment, which saw action in the Civil War starting in November 1862. Almost immediately, he was recruited as colonel to lead the first all-Black regiment, the First South Carolina Volunteers.

"It's better than Prescott's usually are" Louisa wrote this in a letter to family friend, Alf Whitman, Myerson, et al., eds. *Letters*, ed. p. 77.

"My Garden" by Mary Abigail Dodge, Atlantic Monthly, May 1862.

"it would be a relief to end my life." In 1858, when Louisa was desperately trying to find work and begin her writing career, alone in Boston and shortly after her sister Lizzie's death, she tangentially thought of suicide by drowning.

"the sanest man" Thoreau of Bronson Alcott in *Walden*.

"Llewellyn" This is Llewellyn Hovey Willis, who did live with the Alcott's as a boarder over a number of years and, some say, was part of the composite model for Laurie in *Little Women*.

"Walt, the Satyr" From a letter to Abba Alcott, November 13, 1856 in Herrnstadt, R. ed.(1969) *The Letters of A. Bronson Alcott*. Iowa State University Press, p. 210.

"I am the poet of the woman" From Whitman's *Leaves of Grass*, Stanza 21.

"conversation is sublime" From a letter of Emerson to Rev. W. H. Furness in which he also said "I will always love you for loving Alcott." Bonstell, J. and DeForest M. *Little Women Letters from the House of Alcott* Little, Brown & Company, 1914, p. 181.

"Mrs. Hawthorne" At this time, the family of Nathaniel Hawthorne lived next door to the Alcotts. In her diary of Dec. 11, 1862, Sophia Hawthrone wrote about her assistance to Louisa in her preparations to muster out to Washington DC. Diary in Pierrepont Morgan Library, New York City.

"watching the bright instruments . . . smelling bottles" From Louisa's short children's story "Cupid and Chow Chow," 1872.

1863

"Got typhoid fever" From a letter to Alf Whitman, Sept. 1863, Myerson, et al., ds. *Letters*, p. 91.

"Miss Dix and Dr. Channing" Louisa did describe this dream in her Journal for Feb 1863, Myerson, et al., eds. *Journals,* p. 117.

"It's rather solemn . . . small ones" From the short story "Mayflowers" in *A Garland for Girls*, 1888.

"sorrowful failure" Words used by Sylvia in *Moods.*

"may have to pay dearly for the brief exposure" From *Hospital Sketches*, 1863.

"sent his only son to war" This is a line that is often repeated as one Bronson used frequently.

"Ever your admiring rack a bones" The actual valediction Louisa used in her letter to her sister Anna, on the occasion of her firstborn, March 30, 1863, Myerson, et al., eds. *Letters*, p. 83.

"faster than they can be supplied" From Louisa's Journal of April 1863, Myerson, et al., eds. *Journals*, p. 118.

1864

"add this extraordinary power to their natural powers" From Emerson's essay "The Poet."

"the courage of a hero, the eloquence of a poet and the ardor of an Italian." From Louisa's short story "Perilous Play," 1869.

"Mr. Storrs seems like a very gentlemanly D. D." From Louisa's journal of February 1864, Myerson, et al., eds. *Journals*, p.128.

"Mr. Storrs has some connection with Amherst College" Richard Salter Storrs, D.D. (1821–1900) Attended Amherst College (1839), was pastor of the Church of Pilgrims in Brooklyn, as well an author of historical works and, later in life, an associate editor of the *New York Independent*. How the poems of Emily Dickinson appeared in the short-lived paper *The Drumbeat* has never been explained.

"Homer and Milton" The same allusion was made in *Eight Cousins* when Mac suffered his eye ailment.

"Fraternity Festival" was described by Louisa in her June 1864 journal entry, Myerson, et al., eds. *Journals*, p. 130.

"Mr. Alcott is a great man" From a letter of Bronson Alcott to his wife, June 8, 1864, Herrnstadt, R. ed. *The Letters of A. Bronson Alcott*. Iowa State University Press, 1969, p. 356.

"Very little fire…" From *Jo's Boys*.

1865

The reminisces of the Rhine, Coblenz and Goethe's House are from Louisa's journal entries for 1865, Myerson, et al., eds. Journals, p. 142–43.

"Politeness . . . subject" From "Taming a Tartar," 1867.

"empty trunks . . . whole world kin" Paraphrased from *Shawl Straps*, 1872.

"wide low wall, below which lies the lake" From "The Baron's Gloves," 1868.

"He seems nearly restored…face glows" Paraphrased from "My Boys," 1868.

1866

"I begin to think she will outlive me" Anna Weld later married, had a daughter, and lived to the age of eighty-nine.

"There is a young girl…" This is indeed Mabel Loomis Todd, who would go on to be the renowned mistress of Emily's brother, Austin, and also coeditor of the posthumous first edition of Emily's poems. Mabel wrote her reminisces of Concord, where she was born and later spent summers, in a pamphlet, "The Thoreau Family Two Generations Ago," published by the Thoreau Society in 1958.

"I abandoned the notion of genius" Louisa said this in a letter to James Redpath, the publisher of her *Hospital Sketches,* Myerson, et al., eds. *Letters,* p. 103.

"Talent isn't genius" per Jo March in *Little Women.*

1867

"I have developed an oyster-like objection to being torn from my bed" From *Shawl Straps.*

"done nothing for a month but sit in a dark room & ache" From Louisa's journal, January 1867, Myerson, et al., eds. *Journals,* p. 157.

1869

"my arm in a sling and my head wrapped" From a letter to the Lukens Sisters in 1874, Myerson, ed. *Letters,* p. 185.

"stupid style" From a letter in 1869 to her Uncle Samuel May, Myerson, et al., eds. *Letters,* p. 122.

"I say—be you Louiser Alcott?" and "I thought you would be beautiful!" Both anecdotes from an article by Lillie Lucy in *The Cosmopolitan,* 1888.

1870

"own courage, with no guide but our own good sense, three women unprotected except by our Yankee wit" Paraphrased from *Shawl Straps.*

"flurries of snow . . . sirocco" From *Shawl Straps.*

"a dying gladiator" From a letter of Louisa's 1870, Myerson, et al., eds. *Letters,* p.155.

"stiff and stupid" and "dear pious old Fra Angelico suits me better" From *Shawl Straps.*

"You cannot know" From "A Marble Woman," 1865.

"I <u>am</u> glad" from *Shawl Straps.*

"To Boston and Emerson" A cheer spoken by Lavinia, the Louisa character in *Shawl Straps.*

1871

"hold out for a God . . . their temper" Christy Devon says something similar about David Sterling in *Moods.*

"A bookkeeper . . . treadmill" Letter from John Pratt to Alf Whitman in 1870 shortly before his death, from a manuscript in Houghton Library.

"carried his burden . . . cheerfulness" Sentiments expressed in "A Modern Cinderella," Louisa's short story about John and Anna's courtship.

"scribbling a story" Louisa immediately wrote *Little Men,* which was released on the day she arrived back in the States, June 6, 1871.

"something like despair . . . grow any easier" Jo's thoughts after Beth's death in *Little Women.*

"writing splendid work or seeing the world" Beth says something similar to Jo before her death in *Little Women.*

"tug in harness" Louisa used this phrase in her "Recollections from Childhood," written just before her death, 1888.

1872

"I say let woman do whatever she can do" From a letter Louisa wrote to her friend Maria Porter in 1874, Myerson, et al., eds. *Letters*, p. 189.

"I am not a 'rampant women's rights reformer'" From *An Old-Fashioned Girl*, 1869.

"Ho! All ye nervous women folk" From the poem "An Advertisement" by Louisa, printed in *The Woman's Journal*, 1875.

1873

"It is no discredit" From Thomas Wentworth Higginson's assessment of Leaves of Grass in his essay "Literature and Art" published in *Atlantic Monthly*, 1867.

"Kate Field and the Woolsey sisters . . . in a whimsical style" This episode is recounted from Orzeck M., Wesibuch R. *Dickinson and Audience*. University of Michigan Press, 1996, p. 265.

"his literary opinion" Higginson famously misunderstood both Emily's and Louisa's legacy. Just after Louisa's death, in his *Short Stories of American Authors* he wrote of her books: "No mature reader—at least none familiar with literature—cared to keep the run of them."

"Perhaps the whole United States should laugh at me, but what of that?" Emily said something like this to her friends the Hollands in a letter of the summer of 1862. The letters of Emily Dickinson can be accessed online at archive.emilydickinson.org.

1874

"like Goethe, have been putting your joys and sorrows into poems, I turn my adventures into bread and butter" Louisa used this phrase in her journal in April/May 1872, Myerson, et al., eds. *Letters*, p. 182.

"spondulix" Slang for pocket money, used in *Eight Cousins*, 1875.

"Know he was leaving us?" Emily wrote a similar query in a letter to T. W. Higginson on his wife's death, September 1877.

1875

"...never lived much in the world of thoughts" Emily used a similar phrase when describing her mother to T. W. Higginson, April 26, 1862.

"make hay while the sun shines" Louisa said this in a letter to the editor of the *Boston Globe*, Myerson, ed. *Letters*, p. 183.

"I have written a successful book . . . by accident" From *An Old-Fashioned Girl.*

1876

"To meet one of the Thoreau's" This quote is from an obituary clipping of Sophia Thoreau in Yale University Mabel Loomis Todd Collection.

"writing with a kind of indelible ink" From *Rose in Bloom*, 1876.

1877

"never knew . . . human being" From a letter from Elizabeth Peabody to Louisa, quoted in LaPlante, p. 222.

"gentle face and mild dark eyes" From Louisa's very first published story, "The Rival Painters" (1852), a story about a mother's love.

"Last years happy and serene" From *Jo's Boys*, 1886.

"I shall be glad to follow her" From Louisa's journal, November 1877, Myerson, et al., eds. *Journals,* p. 206.

1878

"Helen Hunt is right" Letters exist from Helen Hunt Jackson to Emily urging her to publish in *The Masque of Poets*, an item in the No Name Series, a work published by Roberts Brothers that kept all authors anonymous. There are no letters from Niles to Hunt or Dickinson confirming that Hunt Jackson was the intercessor who had the poem submitted.

"to live, to love, to bless" From the poem "Transfiguration" by Louisa May Alcott, published in the same issue of *The Masque of Poets* as Emily Dickinson's "Success."

"The lovely flowers embarrass me, they make me regret I am not a bee —" From a letter by Emily Dickinson to her Aunt Lucretia in 1864.

1879

"classical humbug" Louisa frequently disparaged the staid and unchanging town of Concord, and used this phrase in a letter shortly before her death, Myerson, et al., eds. *Letters*, p. 338.

"idiots, felons and minors" From a letter of 1881 to Thomas Niles. Myerson, et al, eds. *Letters*, p. 253.

"I mean to go to the polls . . . carry me" Louisa quoted her mother in a letter of 1873 to Lucy Stone, the women's rights activist, Myerson, et al., eds. *Letters*, p. 178.

"enjoy the rights that God gave" From *An Old-Fashioned Girl.*

"It is only the Fourth of July." Emily told this episode and used this exact phrase in a letter of July 1879 to her Norcross cousins.

1880

"I see now why I lived" Louisa said something similar in her own journal for December 1879, Myerson, et al., eds. *Journals*, p. 218.

"So the house would be silent—except for the ghosts." In her journal entry in August 1880, Louisa wrote "the house is full of ghosts." Myerson et al, eds. *Journals*, p. 226.

1882

"sit and listen to my father" Mabel Loomis Todd in her "The Thoreau Family of Two Generations Ago" described an afternoon she spent conversing with Bronson Alcottt, p. 15.

"If one enjoys his own company and pursuits" Paraphrased from Bronson Alcott's *Tablets*.

"to sit serenely in one's soul" From a letter to her Aunt Bond 1887, Myerson, et al., eds. *Letters*, p. 322.

1883

"I have thought you might be…" From a letter from Mrs. Alcott to Louisa, 1843, LaPlante, p. 117.

"Lou Weedy" A pet name used by her nephews.

"There is no light behind the cloud" Contradcits Louisa's quote of the opposite from *Little Women*, chapter 15.

"The memory of all that was sweet and noble . . . still lives" From *Jack and Jill*, 1880.

"to remember his life as a sweet hymn" and "it's blessedness remains" From "Mark Field's Success," 1859.

1884

"I would sing like the boy in the graveyard — to keep the fears away." Emily wrote something similar in a letter to T. W. Higginson, April 1862.

"the curse of a kitchen" Louisa celebrated the lack of a kitchen in her journal, July 1884, Myerson, et al., eds. *Journals*, p. 244.

"make a battering ram of my head" A quote from a letter to her father on their mutual birthday in 1856, Myerson, et al., eds. *Letters*, p. 26.

1885

"I am so busy I have no time to die" Louisa said something similar in letter shortly before her death, Myerson, et al., eds. *Letters*, p. 337.

1886

"infernal end to the March family" *Jo's Boys* was written over seven years and published in July 1886.

"unfinished, the story of May's glorious artist's life" *Diana and Persis* was left unfinished and finally published in partial form in 1978.

"*Wesselhoefts*" the Dickinson's used the services of Dr. William Wesslehoeft, an early homeopath, in the 1850's. Louisa dedicated *Jo's Boys* to Dr. Conrad Wesslehoeft, her longtime physician and the nephew of William.

"the household light and warmth and peace" This aching phrase comes from *Little Women,* when Jo finally brings Mr. Bhaer into the March family home, chapter 23.

"conversation would turn divine" This sentiment was expressed by Louisa in her Civil War story "M.L.," 1863.

"I know how hard it is to spare these dear sisters" and "after the first sharpness of the loss is over" Both are direct quotes from a letter of January 1884 to Maggie Lukans, Myerson, et al., eds. *Letters*, p. 275.

"so slowly refined away that the immortal was shining through by the time she left us" This poignant description is from *Little Women*, describing Beth's illness. Beth was, in fact, Louisa's sister Lizzie.

"stood on the borderland of the spiritual world, ready to return to the mystical place from which she came" Bonstell, J. and DeForest M. *Little Women Letters from the House of Alcott.* Little, Brown & Company, 1914, p. 27.

"going all along" From Emily's poem "Some keep the Sabbath."

"Success is counted sweetest" Arguably Emily's most famous poem, it was printed by Louisa's publisher Thomas Niles, in his *A Masque of Poets.*

"having asked for bread, I got a stone — in the shape of a pedestal." From Louisa's journal of 1875, Myerson, et al., eds. *Journals,* p. 196.

"'Tisn't foolish to be prudent" Vinnie said something similar in a letter to Austin years earlier, October 1, 1851. Bingham, M. (1955) *Emily Dickinson's Home.* Harper and Brothers Publishers.

About the Author

Lorraine Tosiello read Alcott's *Little Women* in the first grade, and again and again most years of her childhood after that. That set her off on her life journey of reading, working as a physician, mother-hood, traveling, and general rabble-rousing. Rereading *Little Women* in later adulthood renewed her Alcott enthusiasm and years of study resulted in her first novel, *Only Gossip Prospers: A Novel of Louisa May Alcott in New York*. She lives with her husband in midtown Manhattan and at the New Jersey shore.

About the Author

Jane Cavolina has been absorbed in a book since her mother signed her up for a book club before she started nursery school. That led to a career in publishing, first as a senior editor at William Morrow, Crown, and Pocket Books, and now as a copyeditor. She is the coauthor of *Growing Up Catholic*, which was on *The New York Times* bestseller list for forty weeks, and other works. She has read every Louisa May Alcott book in the Bayside Public Library with the exception of *Little Women*, and has worn out several copies of *Leaves of Grass*, by her other favorite poet, and cherishes her well-flagged copy of *The Complete Poems of Emily Dickinson*.

Lorraine and Jane were high school friends. Reconnecting forty years later, they found that they were very nearly the spirit of Louisa and Emily in the world today.

ALSO BY CLASH BOOKS

BURIALS

Jessica Drake-Thomas

ALL THE PLACES I WISH I DIED

Crystal Stone

THE SMALLEST OF BONES

Holly Lyn Walrath

WATERFALL GIRLS

Kimberly White

AN EXHALATION OF DEAD THINGS

Savannah Slone

I'M FROM NOWHERE

Lindsay Lerman

HEXIS

Charlene Elsby

HELENA

Claire L. Smith

LA BELLE AJAR

Adrian Ernesto Cepeda

**TRAGEDY QUEENS: STORIES INSPIRED BY
LANA DEL REY & SYLVIA PLATH**

Edited by Leza Cantoral"

CL◀SH

WE PUT THE LIT IN LITERARY

CLASHBOOKS.COM

FOLLOW US

TWITTER

IG

FB

@clashbooks

Advance Praise for *The Bee and the Fly: The Improbable Correspondence of Louisa May Alcott and Emily Dickinson*

In a remarkably convincing rendering, *The Bee and the Fly* imagines a twenty-five year correspondence between two ground-breaking 19th century authors. This novel brilliantly captures the contrasting personalities and distinctive writing cadences of both Louisa May Alcott and Emily Dickinson. Those already well-acquainted with the biographies of these two remarkable women will find few historical inaccuracies in this meticulously-researched novel. Those less familiar will be captivated by the revelations of their experiences and insightful reflections. Either way, you'll come away feeling as if you've just spent a few engaging hours reminiscing with dearly cherished friends.

—Amy Belding Brown, author of *Emily's House, Flight of the Sparrow* and *Mr. Emerson's Wife*

Lorraine Tosiello and Jane Cavolina perfectly embody the voices of Louisa May Alcott and Emily Dickinson through letters between these two world-famous writers. The exquisite writing and intimate details immersed me into the lives of Alcott and Dickinson, leading me to fantasize that the correspondence actually occurred. Don't rush through this book – savor every moment.

—Susan Bailey, curator, *Louisa May Alcott Is My Passion* website

The most delicious literary conceit imaginable - two giants of American nineteenth century women's literature, strangers in real life, begin a secret correspondence that turns into a friendship that turns into a sisterhood. The voice of each rings strong and clear, and whether you're already a fan of one, or both, a historian, a literary detective, or simply someone who cherishes her friends, you are sure to find something to delight you in this thorough treat of a book. Delicious!

—Gabrielle Donnelly, author of *The Little Women Letters*

The Bee & The Fly is an absorbing epistolary novel in which two of the nineteenth century's most beloved women writers exchange their concerns about writing and contemporaneous issues. Framed as an attic discovery, these winsome letters begin in 1861, with Emily Dickinson seeking Louisa May Alcott's advice about her poetry. From initial politesse, they warm into keen displays of the women's opposing personalities. They culminate in the 1880s. . . . The result is a story of impassioned, gentle solidarity that will reward literary fans while inviting more general appreciation for women's friendships. Entertaining in its breadth and intimate about the challenges surrounding writing for publication while longing for greater work, *The Bee & The Fly* is an enchanting flight of fancy centering on two memorable women.

—Karen Rigby, *Foreword Reviews*